VANISHING ACT

When Linda reached the barn, she stopped in the doorway.

"Morning!" she called.

No one answered.

Linda frowned. The barn seemed too quiet. Then she knew why. Amber hadn't answered with her usual nicker of greeting. Linda's heart began to flutter. What if Amber was sick? She hurried down the aisle to the mare's stall. The door was wide open. Linda stared inside. The stall was empty!

"Amber!" she called. She turned and looked into Sheik's stall, and her heart froze.

It was empty, too! The stallion was gone! Both horses had disappeared!

THE LINDA CRAIG ADVENTURES™ #3

THE SILVER STALLION

By Ann Sheldon

A MINSTREL® BOOK

PUBLISHED BY POCKET BOOKS

New York   London   Toronto   Sydney   Tokyo

A MINSTREL PAPERBACK *ORIGINAL*

 A Minstrel Book published by
POCKET BOOKS, a division of Simon & Schuster Inc.
1230 Avenue of the Americas, New York, N.Y. 10020

ISBN: 0-671-64036-4

First Minstrel Books printing September 1988

10 9 8 7 6 5 4 3 2 1

THE LINDA CRAIG ADVENTURES is a trademark of Simon & Schuster Inc.

LINDA CRAIG, A MINSTREL BOOK and colophon are registered trademarks of Simon & Schuster Inc.

Printed in the U.S.A.

1 ♦♦♦♦

"I wish the Duvalls would hurry up and get here," twelve-year-old Linda Craig said to her older brother, Bob. Squinting her brown eyes under her cowboy hat, she peered down Rancho del Sol's long drive. "I'm dying to see Sheik. Bronco says he's the most beautiful Arabian stallion he's ever seen."

"*And* the most expensive," Bob added. He was leaning against the corral fence, his hat pulled low on his forehead.

Linda climbed the fence and sat on the top rail. Amber, her palomino mare, trotted across the corral and nuzzled Linda's pocket.

"No carrots today, girl," Linda said. She smoothed the mare's silky white forelock and patted her golden neck.

Amber reached over and nipped at Bob's cowboy

hat. She caught the brim between her teeth and threw the hat in the air.

"Hey!" Bob hollered. He tried to catch the hat, but it fell in the dust by his feet.

Linda burst out laughing.

"What's so funny?" Her brother pulled a strand of her long dark hair, then waved his arms at Amber. "Get out of here, you pest!"

With a shake of her mane, Amber stepped backward. Then she wheeled, kicked her heels into the air, and raced across the field.

"So much for my new hat," Bob said. He picked up the hat, ran his fingers through his blond hair, and plunked the hat back on his head. "That horse is spoiled rotten," he said.

"No, she's not," protested Linda. "She's just . . ." Suddenly, Linda saw a cloud of dust on the drive. "Hey, look!" She pointed down the drive, which curved in front of the Spanish-style ranch house. "I'll bet that's the Duvalls now."

A moment later, a long white car, followed by an enormous horse van, came into view, passed the house, and stopped in front of Linda and Bob. A tall, handsome man in a western-cut suit stepped out.

"Hello," he said. "I'm Nathan Duvall. You must be Bob and Linda. And this," he continued, as a slender blond girl came around the car to join him, "is my daughter, Page."

"Welcome to Rancho del Sol," Bob said.

"It's nice to meet you." Linda jumped down from the fence and held out her hand.

Nathan greeted her warmly. Page just nodded, then stared over Linda's head as the van pulled around the car and stopped by the barn. "I'm going to unload Sheik," she said to her father.

"I'll help," Bob offered.

Linda watched as her brother took off after Page. Somehow, Page wasn't quite what Linda had expected. She knew Page was her own age, but the girl's expensive-looking denim outfit and short, stylishly cut hair made her appear older. And she wasn't very friendly. Maybe she just wants to make sure her horse arrived safely, Linda thought.

"Hello, Nathan!" a voice said behind her. Tom "Bronco" Mallory, Linda's grandfather, strode around the car. His weathered face broke into a smile. "We thought you took a wrong turn and ended up in the desert!"

Nathan Duvall took Bronco's outstretched hand and shook it warmly. "I didn't dare get lost!" he said. "Page was too eager to get here and start training for Saturday's county horse show. She keeps reminding me it's only a week away."

"Well, she brought her horse to the right place," Bronco said in his deep voice. "I've got an excellent horsewoman here who can help Page get Sheik ready." He put his arm around Linda's shoulder and smiled down at her. Linda smiled back. She and Bob had lived with Bronco and their grandmother, Doña Rosalinda Mallory, ever since the death of their parents several years earlier. Linda and Bob loved their grandparents and had been very happy at Rancho del Sol.

Bronco gave Linda's shoulder a squeeze. "Okay, Nathan," he said. "Let's take a look at that Arabian of your daughter's."

Linda eagerly accompanied the two men to the van, where Page and Bob were waiting at the end of a ramp. The side door of the van was open.

"Bronco, kids, I want you to meet Phil Granger, the best trainer on the West Coast," Nathan said.

A tall, red-haired man inside the van waved.

"Glad to meet you," he said. "Give me a minute to unhitch Sheik and I'll bring him out."

Seconds later, he appeared at the edge of the ramp holding the halter of a huge, muscular, silver gray stallion with a snow white swirl of a cowlick. For a moment, the horse stood as still as a statue. His small ears were pricked forward, and his large brown eyes blinked in the sunlight.

4

"Easy, boy," Phil soothed as he led the horse out of the van.

Stepping carefully on the rubber mat, Sheik made his way down the ramp.

"Whoa!" Phil tugged gently on the lead line.

The stallion halted, and his silky tail fanned out behind him. He stared at the horses in the corral, then gave a loud nicker.

Still holding the lead line, Phil proudly announced, "Presenting Ali Omar Sheik."

"Take off his blanket and leg wraps," Page told him, her eyes sparkling. "Then they can see him better."

Phil pulled off the leg wraps, then unbuckled the lightweight blue cooler and slid it from the horse's back. With a snort, Sheik shied at the fluttering material.

"Let me stand him up," Page said. "I need the practice."

She ran and got a whip from the cab of the van. When she returned, she took the lead line from Phil. She held the whip in the air. Instantly, Sheik arched his neck and stretched his head toward the whip. His muscles rippled. His sleek coat glistened.

"So, what do you think?" Nathan asked.

"He's a fine animal," Bronco said, nodding.

"He's incredible!" Linda agreed as Page tapped Sheik on the hind foot with the whip. Immediately, the horse brought his foot forward.

"That's enough, Page," Phil said quietly. "He's had a long trip."

But Page ignored him and lifted the whip.

"Listen to Phil," Nathan said. "That's why he's here. To make you a better rider, and Sheik a blue-ribbon winner."

"I'm already a good rider," Page grumbled as she handed the lead line to Phil.

"Except you've never worked with a high-spirited stallion like Sheik," her dad said.

"Linda's been schooling her mare for the show, too," Bronco said. "Maybe you girls can help each other."

"Sounds like fun," Linda said, looking at Page. The other girl was staring at the ground.

"Well, you've all had a tiring trip. Let's go on up to the house," Bronco suggested. "Doña's fixing a special dinner."

Nathan glanced at his watch. "Fortunately, I have just enough time for one of Doña's feasts. Then I have to catch a flight back to L.A."

"You're coming back for the show, aren't you, Daddy?" Page shot a pleading look at her father.

"If I can. But you know how busy I am."

"We've fixed a stall for Sheik," Bronco said to Phil. "Bob can help you get him bedded down for the night. Then come on in and join us."

Linda was a little surprised that Page didn't offer to help bed down Sheik, too, but she didn't say anything.

Phil, leading Sheik, followed Bob to the barn. The adults headed for the red-roofed ranch house. Linda stayed behind at the corral with Page. Now that Sheik was safely unloaded, she thought the other girl might want some company.

"So, where's your horse?" Page asked, looking at Linda for the first time.

"In the corral," Linda said. "She's the palomino. Come on, I'll show her to you."

They walked over to the fence, and Linda whistled. Amber lifted her head, pricked her small ears, and nickered softly. In the glow of the setting sun, her coat shone like a nugget of gold.

With a playful toss of her head, Amber trotted over to the fence, her hooves daintily skimming the grass. She nuzzled Linda's arm.

"She's nice," Page said absently. Then she turned her head and looked at her father as he walked up the drive. Turning back to Amber, she reached out a hand and began to stroke the mare's neck. There was a sad expression on Page's face.

7

"I hope your dad can make it to the show," Linda said, trying to make Page feel better.

Page shrugged her shoulders. "He'll be happy if I win a blue ribbon in the Park Horse class," she said. Then her face brightened. "You should see the outfit he bought me. The coat's lilac, and the derby has a hatband to match."

"That's nice," Linda replied as enthusiastically as possible. She'd watched Park Horse class competitions before, and had thought that the gaits of the horses looked artificial.

"What classes are you riding in?" Page asked.

"Just the ones for local riders," Linda said. "Amber isn't a purebred, like an Arabian, so she can't go in the others."

"Oh, that's too bad." Page shook her head. "Arabians are the best breed there is!"

Linda disagreed, but she didn't think it would be polite to say so. Page *was* her guest.

"Want to see the barn?" Linda said instead. "I've got to bed Amber down for the night."

"Nope. Too hungry. I'll see you at dinner," Page said and ran off to catch up with her father.

Linda walked to the corral gate and unlatched it to let Amber out. The mare pushed the gate open with her nose. She walked through, then turned and pushed the gate shut.

Linda laughed at Amber's latest trick. Page might think Arabians were the best, but as far as Linda was concerned, no one could compete with Amber.

"Come on. Let's put you in your stall." Lightly, Linda laid her hand on Amber's mane and together they walked to the barn.

Tomorrow, Linda thought, I'll invite Page for a ride. Then we can get to know each other better.

But at breakfast the next morning, Page wasn't too thrilled when Linda mentioned a ride.

"The show is in six days," Page said. "I can't spend time galloping around the ranch."

"But Rancho del Sol is just about the biggest ranch in Southern California," Linda said. "You really should see it while you're here. It covers thousands of acres, and there are tons of really great trails to ride on."

"I told you, I don't have time to ride around your ranch," Page said, unimpressed. "Besides, Sheik's not a trail horse." She took one last gulp of orange juice and stood up. "Anyway, don't you have to school Amber?"

"I can do that on the trail," Linda said.

"Well, I can't. A good show horse needs a ring. I'm giving Sheik a workout this morning. Why don't you come and watch?"

"Great," Linda muttered at Page's departing back. "That'll *really* be fun."

"I guess she told you," Bob said, striding into the kitchen. "And she's right. You haven't worked Amber much in the ring. She'll probably buck you off at the show."

"She will not," Linda snapped.

"Hey! I was just teasing. You don't have to get mad."

"Sorry. It's just that everyone's so worried about winning ribbons. What's the big deal?"

Bob poured some juice. "If you owned a horse that cost as much as Sheik, you'd worry, too."

Linda shook her head. "Then I'm glad I don't. Anyway, he's not all that perfect. Did you see his hooves? They're narrow and pointy."

"They shoe Arabian show horses that way," Bob said with a laugh. He ruffled Linda's long hair.

Linda ducked from his hand. Bob was only three years older than she was, and she hated it when he treated her like a kid. "How was I supposed to know? None of the Arabian horses on the ranch are shod like that."

"That's because we don't show them in Park Horse classes. The long hoof makes the horses pick up their feet really high."

Linda wrinkled her nose. "That's what makes them trot that way?"

He nodded. Linda watched him pile his plate high with scrambled eggs, toast, and bacon.

"You'll get fat," she teased as she grabbed two apples from the fruit bowl on the table and dumped a handful of sugar lumps into her pocket.

"So will that horse of yours," Bob replied.

Linda ignored his teasing. "Tell Doña I'm going out on Amber. Page may not be interested in a trail ride, but I sure am."

"Have a good time," Bob said between bites.

But halfway to the barn, Linda decided to see what Page and her horse could do.

Mac, the ranch foreman, was leaning against the fence, watching the workout in the riding ring. He looked sleepy, but Linda knew he was keenly observing every detail of the workout.

"That's a mighty good-looking animal," Mac said as Linda joined him.

"He sure is," Linda agreed. Shading her eyes from the sun, she peered over the fence.

Sheik stood in the middle of the ring with Page on his back. Phil was holding on to the English bridle. He pointed to the rail and said something to Page. Then he let go of the bridle. Page urged Sheik forward. Linda thought she was holding the reins awfully tight.

"Just go easy," Phil called from the middle of the ring. "Remember, Sheik is more sensitive than the horses you're used to riding. Be calm and gentle when you signal him."

Page squeezed her legs against the horse's side. The stallion began to trot. She posted, moving up and down in the English saddle in rhythm with the horse. Sheik began to move more quickly.

"Talk to him," Phil called again. "Tell him to go slow and easy."

Sheik trotted along the rail toward Linda and Mac. Page pulled on the reins, trying to turn him in a circle.

"She's a bit heavy-handed with that horse," Mac commented. "But Phil's a good trainer—he'll be able to teach her how to handle Sheik."

"Just like you taught me how to handle Amber," Linda replied, smiling at Mac.

"I want to work on the park trot!" Page yelled to Phil as Sheik trotted past him.

"Hold on," he said. "One thing at a time."

But Page was already urging Sheik on. She held the reins high and squeezed harder with her calves. The stallion's hooves reached up and out, then pounded into the ground. He stormed past Linda and Mac, kicking up a cloud of dust.

"Whew!" Linda said, coughing.

"Crazy things they make show horses do." Mac grinned. "Give me an old cow pony any day."

"Slow him down!" Phil shouted, starting to lose his patience. "He's overexcited."

But Page didn't hear, or didn't feel like listening. Trying to get the stallion to lift his feet higher, she tapped him on the flank with the riding whip. Confused, the young horse broke into a canter. Page pulled on the reins, but Sheik only went faster.

Linda could see the whites of the stallion's eyes. There was a frightened look on Page's face as she clung to the saddle.

"Whoa, Sheik!" Phil called anxiously.

Suddenly, Linda heard a nicker behind her. She turned and saw Amber peering around the corner of the barn. Ears pricked with curiosity, the mare began to trot toward the ring.

"Oh, no!" Linda groaned. "Amber's let herself out again!"

"Better catch her," Mac warned. "Page is having enough trouble with that stallion without Amber spooking him."

Linda took off at a run toward the mare.

"Stop," she said to Amber. But with a frisky toss of her mane, Amber pranced out of reach. Linda knew the mare was only playing. But she couldn't let her scare Sheik!

"Stop!" she commanded more firmly.

This time Amber stopped dead in her tracks. Linda ran up and grasped the mare's halter.

But it was too late!

Sheik had caught sight of the loose horse running outside the ring. His head flew up, and his nostrils flared with excitement. He spun in a circle, throwing Page onto his neck, then headed toward the fence at a wild gallop.

Linda gasped. He was going to jump!

2 ♦♦♦♦

"Oh, no!" Linda cried, grasping Amber's halter even tighter.

Now Sheik was heading straight for Mac.

Quickly but calmly, Mac stepped onto the lowest fence board and raised his arms in the air.

Startled, the stallion veered away. Page yanked the reins and managed to turn the horse. But then Sheik ducked his head and bucked. Thrown off balance, Page fell onto his neck.

Mac vaulted over the fence. He and Phil reached Sheik at the same time. "Whoa!" Mac and Phil shouted in unison.

The stallion slid to an abrupt halt. With a surprised cry, Page tumbled over the horse's neck. She landed on the ground with a thud.

Mac grabbed Sheik's bridle. Phil ran to Page. She was lying still, a stunned look on her face.

"Are you hurt?" Phil asked anxiously.

Linda led Amber to the fence. "Is Page okay?" she called.

Ignoring their concern, Page jumped up. "Why is that horse running loose!" she screamed. "I could have broken my neck!"

"I'm sorry," Linda said. "Are you all right?"

"I'm just great," Page said sarcastically, slapping at the dust on her pants. She glared at Linda, then motioned toward Amber. "From now on, just keep that horse locked up!" she snapped.

Page picked up her whip from the ground and waved it. It had broken in the middle, and one end dangled uselessly. "My new whip!" she wailed.

"Forget the whip," Phil said. He was stroking Sheik's sweaty neck, trying to soothe the nervous stallion. "The important thing is you're not hurt. Now, hop back into the saddle, and this time, pay attention."

Without replying, Page mounted Sheik again.

Embarrassed that Amber had caused so much trouble, Linda apologized again. Then she turned the mare toward the barn.

Mac let go of Sheik's bridle and went after Linda.

"Don't be so hard on yourself," he said, when he caught up to her. "The way that horse was acting, anything would've set him off."

"But it *was* Amber's fault," Linda said. "And Page could have been hurt."

"The only thing that girl hurt was her pride," Mac stated. "Still, I'd better put a new latch on Amber's door. Then if Page falls off again, she can't blame it on your horse!" He winked and strode off toward the machine shed.

Linda turned to Amber. "You really caused a lot of trouble today," she scolded. The palomino hung her head. Laughing, Linda hugged her.

"Come on, you faker. Let's go on that trail ride. Page isn't the only one who has to practice for the show!"

Saturday, the day of the horse show, came quickly. Linda and Page had worked hard with their horses all week. But after the accident in the riding ring, Page had barely spoken to Linda.

Linda wasn't sure if Page was still mad about Amber spooking Sheik, or if she was just concerned about getting her high-spirited horse ready for the show.

But today, Linda had decided not to worry about it. There was too much to do.

"Don't let me forget my good chaps," Linda told Bronco as he carried her western saddle into the horse van. He set the saddle on the saddle rack.

Linda draped her bridle over a hook and plunked a bucket of brushes on the floor. "And my dark blue cowboy hat," she added.

Bronco grinned. "As excited as you two girls have been, I'm surprised you didn't pack up the van days ago."

"I wanted to, but Page . . ." Linda's voice trailed off.

Bronco put his arm around her shoulders. "Don't be too hard on Page," he said quietly. "Her mother died when she was a baby. She's only got her father, and he's away on business a lot."

"I guess," Linda said. "It's too bad he can't come to the show. She's very disappointed."

Just then, Bob puffed up the ramp carrying a bale of hay. "Where do you want this?" he asked.

"Here." Linda pointed to a small area close to the front of the van. The area was separated from the rest of the van by a wooden partition. "I'll sit on it. I volunteered to ride in back, near the horses."

Bob shoved the bale behind the partition, then looked around. "Wow, this rig is really great. It has a tack room *and* a dressing room."

"It is a nice rig," Bronco agreed. He clapped Bob on the back. "Now let's help load the horses so the show riders can get going!"

A moment later, Phil arrived to lend a hand with the horses. When they were safely inside the van, he got into the cab behind the wheel. Page and Bob climbed into the van beside him.

"Doña and I will see you at the show," Bronco called, as he waved them on their way.

Soon they were heading down the highway toward Lockwood, the closest town to Rancho del Sol. Sponsored by the 4-H club, the horse show was being held at the fairground just outside of town.

In the van, Amber and Sheik were stabled side by side. They nipped playfully at each other and bit from the net of hay hanging between them.

Linda, safely behind the partition, smiled at their antics. She reached up and stroked Sheik's soft nose. He really was a nice horse. If only he'd win a ribbon for Page and her father. Maybe then Page could relax and enjoy him more.

After the van pulled into the fairground and parked, Linda quickly unloaded Amber and got to work. She was entered in the first class.

"This is it," she said, slipping the halter from the mare's head. Amber's ears flicked back and forth as she stared at all the strange sights. Quietly, Linda tacked her up, soothing her with calm words as she adjusted the palomino's saddle and bridle. She rubbed Amber's glossy coat with a towel, then brushed the last tangle from her tail. Suddenly, Linda heard the loudspeaker crackle.

"All entries for Western Pleasure, please come to the ring," called the announcer.

With a deep breath, Linda bent down and wiped the dust from her boots. Then she mounted. Phil and Bob wished her good luck, and as she walked Amber toward the ring, she knew she'd need it. The class may have been for local owners, but that didn't mean the competition wouldn't be tough.

Linda steered Amber into the crowded ring and joined the other riders. She tried to remember what Bronco had told her that morning.

"Stay on the rail, keep away from the other horses, and relax," he'd said.

Relax. That was the hardest. Already she had butterflies in her stomach.

Linda closed her eyes and pictured her favorite trail. She could see it clearly—the desert wildflowers, cactus, a roadrunner. When she opened her eyes, the butterflies were gone.

"Okay, girl," she whispered to Amber. "Let's show 'em."

"Walk, please," the ringmaster said.

Linda found an open spot on the rail. Amber stared wide-eyed at the people hanging over the fence. But when Linda gave her a loving pat, the mare seemed to settle down.

"Jog, please," the ringmaster said.

Linda sat deep in the saddle. She squeezed Amber lightly with her heels. The mare began a slow trot, so smooth that Linda barely moved in the saddle.

"Lope, please."

Linda signaled Amber. Instantly she stretched out her legs, speeding up to a steady canter.

So far, so good, thought Linda, as she guided Amber back to the ringmaster. Amber was performing so well, maybe they'd win third, or even second place.

The ringmaster asked the riders to walk, reverse and walk, jog, and lope in the other direction. When all the horses were lined up in the center, Linda wanted to hug Amber. She'd performed like a dream, quietly following each of Linda's commands like a perfect Western Pleasure horse. Linda was really proud of her.

Linda looked over at the crowd behind the fence and saw Doña and Bronco smiling at her. She smiled back at them and gave a little wave.

Then the ringmaster cleared his throat.

"First place goes to number four-oh-four, Amber, owned and ridden by Miss Linda Craig."

The crowd began to applaud. Linda couldn't believe it! A blue ribbon at her first show! She urged Amber forward. The mare greeted the judge as if they were old friends. With the blue ribbon fluttering from Amber's bridle, they left the ring. Linda was grinning from ear to ear. Then she saw Page, mounted on Sheik, waiting to enter the ring for the next class. Page wore the lilac-colored coat and the derby she'd told Linda about.

"Congratulations," Page said.

"Thanks!" Linda replied with a proud smile.

"Too bad it was just a class for local horses," Page added. "I'd like to see what you'd do with some real competition." She tapped Sheik with her whip, and they jogged into the ring.

"Don't listen to her," Linda muttered to Amber. "She's just jealous."

Just then, Phil came up beside them. "Great job!" he said with a grin. "You two looked like real pros." He craned his neck, trying to see Sheik over the other horses. The stallion was already trotting up the side of the ring, tossing his head and snorting nervously. Page held tightly to the reins, trying to make him walk.

The grin faded from Phil's face as he watched Page and Sheik.

"They both look nervous," Linda said. "At least I know *I* was."

Phil nodded. "They're *too* nervous, if you ask me," he said. Then he shook his head. "I tried to tell Page's father that neither of them was ready for the show." He walked over to the rail to get a better view. Linda steered Amber beside him.

"Trot, please," the ringmaster said.

Linda figured there were about fifteen horses in the class. But still, she had no trouble spotting Page and Sheik. The stallion was cantering instead of trotting.

And Page was only making things worse. Instead of trying to soothe him, she was jerking hard on his mouth and flopping in the saddle. Not knowing how to regain control, Page swatted Sheik with her whip to make him obey her.

The stallion responded to the sting of the whip by bursting past a group of horses. He galloped into the middle of the ring, almost running over the judge. The ringmaster waved at Page, then he frowned and pointed to the gate.

Phil shook his head. "Oh, no," he groaned. "They're kicking her out of the class."

Red-faced with embarrassment, Page managed to turn Sheik around. He snorted nervously as she led him up to the gate. Phil opened the gate. As Sheik started through, two horses crowded behind him. He reared, flinging his head into the air, and lunged forward. The reins slid from Page's grasp, and the stallion bolted through the gate and headed straight for a crowd of people.

Without stopping to think, Linda turned Amber toward Sheik. The mare leaped forward, cutting between the runaway stallion and the crowd. Amber pushed against Sheik's side, forcing him into the railing around the ring. Sheik stopped. Phil ran up to the stallion and grabbed hold of his bridle.

Page leaned over and snatched the reins from Phil's hand.

"I could have stopped him!" she snapped at Linda. "You didn't have to act like this was some cow-cutting contest."

"Page!" Phil said sternly. "You should thank Linda and Amber. They kept Sheik from hurting someone."

"Thank you!" Page said in a haughty tone, and, jumping off Sheik, she stormed away.

Phil and Linda looked at each other.

"Sorry about Page's behavior," Phil said.

"I guess she's upset about getting dismissed from the class," Linda replied.

"That was kind of rough. Page just doesn't understand that it takes time to train a good show horse. Especially when the horse is as sensitive and spirited as Sheik." Phil stroked the horse's silver neck. The stallion nuzzled his cheek.

"He seems to really like you," Linda said.

Phil nodded. "I've worked with him ever since he was a foal. With the right training, he'll make a super horse. I just wish . . ." His voice trailed off. "Well, I think he's had enough." He pulled the reins over Sheik's head.

"Amber and I have one more class," Linda said. "It's Barrel Racing. Bob and Rocket are competing in it, too. But after that, Amber and I will be happy to keep Sheik company."

When the Barrel-Racing class was over, Linda was pretty sure that she and Amber weren't going to win a ribbon. But she knew that they had done the best they could in the event. Linda's small feeling of disappointment was replaced by a rush of pleasure when the ringmaster announced that the blue ribbon was going to Bob and his bay gelding.

Bob and Linda left the ring and dismounted. Bronco and Doña walked up to them.

"Congratulations to you both," Doña said, her dark eyes sparkling. She hugged Linda, then Bob. "And congratulations to Amber and Rocket, too," she added with a smile.

"How about some lunch?" suggested Bronco. "You two blue-ribbon winners must be hungry."

"Not hungry," Linda said. *"Starving!"*

After a quick lunch, Linda walked through the parked trailers and trucks searching for Phil. He'd promised to help her load Amber in the van.

As she came around a pickup truck, she spied him talking to two men.

"Sheik is a beautiful animal," she heard Phil say.

Then he saw her and waved.

Linda waved back. "We're ready to load!" she called.

Phil nodded. Linda turned and made her way to the Duvalls' van. She had to agree with the trainer—Sheik was a beautiful animal. But beauty didn't win ribbons. And winning seemed to be the only thing that would make Page happy.

Sunday morning, Linda woke up at six o'clock. The house was quiet.

For a moment, she lay in bed thinking about the day before. After the show, Page hadn't said a word. She'd barely eaten anything at dinner, and afterward, she'd gone straight to her room. Later, when her father phoned the ranch, she had refused to talk to him.

Linda felt sorry for her. Page had had her heart set on winning, which must have made getting kicked out of the class twice as embarrassing. No wonder she hadn't wanted to talk to her dad.

As far as Linda was concerned, Page was missing the whole point of owning a horse. She cared so much about winning blue ribbons, she wasn't having any fun with Sheik. And to Linda, having fun with a horse was the best thing about owning one.

Yawning, Linda slid out of bed. She pulled on a T-shirt, jeans, and cowboy boots. She'd feed Sheik and Amber early. Then, after breakfast, she'd ask Page again about a trail ride.

Paintbrush Valley might be fun, Linda thought. And it was an easy trail. There weren't any holes or sharp rocks for Page to worry about.

The morning was clear and crisp. Linda walked briskly to the barn. Halfway there, she noticed that the barn door was wide open.

"That's funny," she murmured. "Someone must be up already." She knew that was unusual. Sunday mornings, even Mac slept late.

When Linda reached the barn, she stopped in the doorway.

"Morning!" she called.

No one answered.

Linda frowned. The barn seemed too quiet. Then she knew why. Amber hadn't answered with her usual nicker of greeting.

Linda's heart began to flutter. What if Amber was sick?

27

She hurried down the aisle to the mare's stall. The door was wide open. Linda stared inside. The stall was empty!

"Amber!" she called. She turned and looked into Sheik's stall, and her heart froze.

It was empty, too! The stallion was gone!

3 ♦♦♦♦

Both horses had disappeared!

Linda couldn't believe it. There had to be some explanation. Maybe one of the ranch hands had moved them to different stalls.

She ran down the aisle. She passed Rocket; Mac's quarterhorse, Buck; Bronco's stallion, Colonel; and Nacho, the family's old pony.

But there was no sign of Amber or Sheik.

Don't panic, Linda told herself. Maybe Mac turned them out in one of the corrals.

Running out of the barn, Linda scanned the corral and the riding ring. Both were empty. She raced around the barn to the smaller corral. She saw only two ranch horses, who whinnied hungrily.

Now Linda was really worried. Could Amber and Sheik be in the horse-breaking ring?

"Oh, let them be there!" she whispered.

But the ring was empty. She climbed the fence and peered across the pasture.

Suddenly, she heard a nicker, and a flash of gold behind the cow barn caught her eye. Amber. The palomino trotted out from behind the barn, a clump of grass hanging from her mouth.

"Amber!" Linda cried with relief.

At the sound of Linda's voice, the mare jogged up to her. Linda gave her a quick hug. Now, where was Sheik?

Leading Amber by the halter, Linda checked the cow barn. It was cool and dark.

"Sheik?" she called. But there was no answering whinny.

Frowning, Linda walked Amber back into the sunlight.

"Let's put you in your stall," she said. "Then I've got to get Mac."

Sheik had to be nearby, she told herself. Mac would know where to look.

Linda led Amber to her stall and tossed her some hay. Then she ran to the bunkhouse and tapped gently on Mac's door.

"Mac?" she called softly.

"Yeah? What is it?" came a voice from inside. A

moment later, Mac opened the door. He was wearing a T-shirt and jeans. "What's wrong?" he asked when he saw Linda's worried expression.

"Sheik's missing!"

"What!" The ranch foreman's eyes widened.

"He's not in his stall. I've looked everywhere."

"Hold on. I'll be out in a second." Mac disappeared inside.

While she waited, Linda paced the wooden porch. They had to find Sheik!

Mac reappeared, his shirt in his hand. "Now, tell me the whole story," he said, slipping the shirt on as they walked down the porch steps.

Linda told him about the open barn door, the empty stalls, and finding Amber. "I even checked the cow barn," she added.

Mac frowned. "I closed the door of the horse barn myself. About eleven o'clock last night."

"Do you think someone might have moved him?" Linda asked.

"Not that I know of." He patted her on the shoulder. "Now, don't get too worked up. Sheik's got to be around here somewhere."

They searched around the ranch house and the machine shed. Then Mac got the jeep, and they drove into the pasture next to the barns. A group of colts, startled by the jeep, cantered away from them. But there was no sign of Sheik.

By this time, Mac was puzzled.

Finally, they agreed, they had to get help. But they both knew that meant telling Phil and Page that the valuable horse was missing.

Linda and Mac found everyone gathered in the large kitchen. Bob was yawning sleepily. Luisa, the Mallorys' cook and housekeeper, was taking corn-bread from the oven. Doña was standing in front of the kitchen table, pouring coffee for the adults. Her dark, shining hair was pulled back neatly into a bun. There was a calm expression on her pretty face.

Even early on a Sunday morning, Linda thought, Doña looks ready to deal with anything. It was a comforting feeling.

"Sheik's gone!" Page cried, after Mac had told her and the others the news. "But where?" She turned to Phil, a bewildered expression on her face. "Did you move him?" she asked the trainer.

Phil shook his head. "No. I checked him last night and he was fine."

"Then what happened to him?" Page demanded, looking around the kitchen at everyone.

Bronco held up his hand to silence her. "I want to hear Linda's story."

Linda repeated it. Mac filled in the rest. As they talked, Bronco nodded thoughtfully.

"He's got to be somewhere on the ranch," he said, when Linda and Mac had finished. "He probably headed out behind the barns into the lush pasture. When the horses are finished feeding, we'll saddle up and go after him."

"When they finish feeding!" Page exclaimed. "We need to go *now!* There's no telling what could happen to Sheik!"

Bronco put his hand on her shoulder. "I know you're worried, Page. But there's no use starving our horses. I'll bet Sheik's found a nice field full of green grass and he's as happy as can be. Now, how about some of that cornbread, Luisa."

"But, but . . ." Page sputtered.

"Bronco's right," Phil said. "We need to stay calm. Sheik will be fine."

Page glared at everyone. "You all just don't care, do you?" she yelled and left the kitchen.

Linda started after her. But Phil put a hand on her arm to stop her.

"Page needs to cool off a little," he said.

"I guess you're right," replied Linda. "It's just that I understand how terrible she feels. I was scared to death when I couldn't find Amber."

"Oh, yes." He chuckled. "The Houdini of the horse world. She certainly has gotten Sheik into a lot of trouble."

"What do you mean?"

"Well, it's pretty clear to me that she let him out of his stall."

Linda stared at Phil in disbelief.

"How else did Sheik get out?" Phil continued.

"I don't know how he got out," Linda replied. "But it wasn't Amber's fault. She only lets herself out, not other horses."

"There's always a first time," Bob said behind her, his mouth full of cornbread.

Linda turned sharply. "It wasn't Amber. I just know it. Besides, yesterday Mac put a new lock on her stall."

Phil set his coffee mug down. "So? She's plenty smart. She probably spent all night figuring out how to get it open. Then she let Sheik out."

"Everyone ready?" Bronco interrupted before Linda could respond. Phil and Bob nodded. Bronco handed Phil a road map, which included Rancho del Sol and the area around it. "Phil, you take the jeep and check the road. Mac, you and Bob and I will ride out to the winter pasture."

"I'll call the neighbors," Doña said. "Maybe one of them has spotted Sheik."

"What about me?" a voice asked.

Page stood in the kitchen doorway. She wore yellow britches and high black boots. Her eyes looked red, as if she'd been crying.

"It's important that you and Linda stay here in case Sheik comes back on his own," Bronco told her. "And you two can keep searching around here. There are still lots of places he could be."

"But I want to ride with you!" Page insisted.

"Me, too!" Linda said. She knew Amber would be a big help. Besides, she didn't want to be left behind.

"No," Bronco said firmly. "If Sheik does come back, and he's hurt, he'll respond much better to you, Page. He doesn't know any of the ranch hands." He turned to the others. "Let's get going."

The men filed out. Doña went into the study to call the neighbors.

"You girls are much better off staying here," Luisa said. "There's no telling what could happen out there on those trails." She smiled brightly. "Now, how about some nice, hot cornbread?"

"No thanks," Linda said. She left the kitchen feeling really disappointed. Bronco had never left her out like this before. Maybe he figured she'd better stay behind in case Page needed help. *If* Sheik showed up. Linda doubted that he would.

A second later, Linda heard the door slam.

"Hey, wait up!" Page called.

Linda slowed down to let Page catch up to her.

"I can't believe this," the blond girl grumbled as she fell into step beside Linda. "Sheik's *my* horse. I should be out there looking for him."

For once Linda agreed with her. But she felt she had to defend her grandfather. "Bronco's right, Page. Someone needs to stay behind in case Sheik comes back."

"*You* could have stayed alone! After all, it's *your* horse's fault!"

Linda stopped in her tracks. "What do you mean by that?"

"I heard Phil. He said Amber unlocked her door, then let Sheik out. And now he's lost!"

Page shouted the last two words, then turned and raced the rest of the way to the barn.

Linda just watched her go. She'd about had it with Page.

All week long, she'd been friendly and polite to her guest. And what had Page done in return? Ignored her and worried about the show. And she had the nerve to accuse Amber!

Well, Linda thought, it's about time someone told Page Duvall what a spoiled brat she was!

Fists clenched, Linda marched down the drive to

the barn. She stopped in the wide aisle between the stalls. Page was nowhere in sight. She listened. All she could hear was the rustling and munching of hay as the horses ate.

Then she heard another sound. Someone was crying.

Quietly, Linda tiptoed past Amber's stall to Sheik's. She peered over the door.

Page was huddled in the fresh straw, her head on her arms. Her shoulders shook with sobs.

"Page?" Linda called softly. "Are you okay?"

The girl's sobs only grew louder.

Linda opened the door and walked in. She sat in the straw next to Page. The stall smelled like freshly baled hay and sweet feed.

"I'm really sorry about Sheik," Linda said. "But don't worry. They'll find him."

Page continued to cry. Linda reached over and gently patted her on the shoulder. The girl shrugged her hand away.

"You don't really care," she sobbed. "No one does. And now my plans are ruined."

"We *do* care," Linda said gently. "Sheik will probably be back in his stall by dinnertime. That'll give you lots of time to ride him."

"But Mr. Greene is coming here this morning!" Page looked up. Tears streaked her cheeks.

"Mr. Greene?" Linda asked, puzzled, though the name did sound familiar to her. "Who's he?"

"He's *the* top Arabian trainer in the state." Page dried her eyes with the back of her hand. "And yesterday at the show he came up to *me!* Can you believe it?"

Almost magically, her tears disappeared.

"What did he want?" Linda asked.

"To buy Sheik! He wanted to talk to my dad. But I told him we weren't interested in selling."

"Oh." Linda nodded. Now she remembered where she'd heard the man's name before. Bronco had mentioned him just last week. And he hadn't said very nice things about him. Linda knew that if Bronco didn't like someone, there was usually a good reason.

"After I told him Sheik wasn't for sale, he still wanted to come and see him," Page continued. "And he wants to talk to *me* about training with him."

Page's eyes filled with tears again. "Only now I'll have to call and tell him Sheik's gone!"

"Maybe he can come out another time," Linda suggested.

Page shook her head sadly. "He's leaving this afternoon for a big horse show. I'll never have another chance to talk to him."

With a sigh, Linda wrapped her arms around her

legs. She certainly hadn't done a very good job of cheering up her guest.

"I'm sorry your plans got messed up," she said.

"I'll bet you are." Page scowled. "Ever since I got here you've tried to ruin things. And I think it's because you're jealous. In fact, I think you're so jealous that *you* let Sheik out!"

4 ◆◆◆◆

Linda's mouth fell open. She stared at Page. The blond girl turned away. Her shoulders were stiff with anger.

Linda didn't know what to say. Page was accusing *her* of letting Sheik out!

"That's crazy," she said finally. "Why would *I* let Sheik out?"

Page whirled around to face Linda. "Because you don't like me!"

Page's words took Linda by surprise. "What do you *mean* I don't like you? I've tried hard to make friends with you."

"Oh, sure," Page said, jumping to her feet. "All you've done is ask me on some dumb old trail ride. You never asked what I wanted to do."

"That's because all you're interested in is winning ribbons!"

They glared at each other.

Then Linda sighed. "Look, Page. I didn't let Sheik out. And neither did Amber. It's not our fault."

"Well, if you didn't, then who did?"

Linda had no answer. Who would let a prize stallion like Sheik out of his stall? It couldn't have been anyone at Rancho del Sol!

"I don't know," she said, getting to her feet. "But I'm going to find out."

She left the stall and walked into the tack room. Maybe a ride would help her think. She'd stay close by the ranch in case Sheik returned.

She carried her saddle to Amber's stall and swung it onto the door. Page had left, which was just as well. Linda didn't want to get into another argument with her.

As Linda opened the mare's door, she checked the new latch. She pushed the bolt back and forth several times.

It was as she'd thought. There was no way Amber could have used her teeth and lips to get the latch open. It was too tricky.

Linda fed the palomino a carrot, then brushed the dust from her glossy coat. Amber's muscles tensed with excitement when she saw the saddle. She was ready to go!

Linda pulled the bridle from the saddle horn.

Amber lowered her head so Linda could slip the bit into her mouth and smooth her forelock under the brow band. Next, Linda pulled the saddle from the door and gently flung it onto the blanket she'd placed on Amber's back. Then she tightened the girth.

When the mare pushed the door open with her nose, Linda had to laugh. "I think you're ready for a ride!"

They walked from the barn, and Linda mounted.

Amber didn't need any coaxing. Linda had to hold her to a walk as they passed the machine shed and headed into a grove of walnut trees. Then she allowed Amber to break into a jog.

The trail was cool and quiet. The sun, shining between the leaves, made dancing shadows. Amber's ears flicked back and forth as she looked curiously at everything.

Linda took a deep breath. This was riding!

They jogged through the trees and down a slope toward a wide stream. Near the edge, Amber hesitated, and Linda slowed her to a walk. The mare stepped carefully down the muddy bank of the stream and into the rushing, knee-deep water.

"Good girl," Linda said, patting the horse's golden neck.

Amber sloshed halfway across, then stopped to put her head down to drink. Linda glanced around.

Suddenly, water splashed onto her arms and legs. Amber was pawing playfully in the stream.

"Hey!" Linda protested. She was getting soaked.

She pulled the mare's head up and gave her a gentle kick. The palomino lunged across the stream and up the bank. Linda halted her.

"I didn't need a bath!" Laughing, Linda wiped her face with her shirt. Shaking like a dog, Amber dried herself off. Then she continued along the trail as if nothing had happened.

As they jogged along the winding stream, Linda began to think about Page's question. Who had let the horses out?

Both Phil and Mac had checked the stall doors, and Mac had closed up the barn. After inspecting the latch, Linda was positive it couldn't have been Amber. Besides, the mare was smart, but there was no way she could have opened the big barn door. So the culprit had to be human.

But who?

And why? Why would someone let a pampered horse like Sheik loose on the open range?

All of a sudden, Amber stopped so quickly that Linda fell forward onto the saddle horn. She grabbed the horse's mane to keep from falling off.

Amber was standing as still as a statue. Her ears

were pricked forward. Her nostrils quivered as she stared into a thick grove of pines.

Shading her eyes, Linda looked in the same direction. She heard a rustle of leaves. Then she saw the shadow of a large shape moving through the underbrush.

Could it be Sheik?

"Come on, girl, let's go see," Linda said, urging Amber forward.

Hesitantly, the mare took a step. A twig snapped. Amber snorted but stood her ground. Linda stroked her neck, then clucked. They moved closer, and Linda leaned forward, trying to see what was in the brush.

Suddenly, a mule deer burst through the trees and raced down the path. Linda and Amber jumped in surprise. The mare wheeled around on her hindquarters, then stopped abruptly. She stared after the fleeing deer. Linda laughed, but her heart was pounding.

"Whew!" she said, wiping her brow. Then she reached over and gave Amber a pat. "Good girl," she told the mare. "You didn't shy. I'm really proud of you."

Then she pointed to the ground. "If we'd looked closer, we would have known it wasn't Sheik. Look at the deer prints."

It was too bad it wasn't Sheik, Linda thought as she turned Amber toward the ranch. But even if they had found Sheik, Linda doubted whether Page would stop believing that Linda had let him out. Somehow, she had to convince Page that neither she nor Amber had had anything to do with Sheik's disappearance. But to do that, Linda had to find out who really was responsible.

Suddenly Linda thought of Mr. Greene. Maybe he was another piece to the puzzle of Sheik's disappearance. How badly had he wanted the horse?

He knew that the stallion was at the ranch. Had he sneaked into the barn and let the horse out? A trainer like Mr. Greene would know that wandering around on the range would really hurt Sheik's condition. Maybe enough so that Page and her father would think again about selling him. After all, Mr. Greene and everyone else at the show knew Page couldn't handle the horse. If the stallion looked terrible, too, the Duvalls just might want to get rid of him.

But why would Mr. Greene let Amber out?

As she rode to the barn, Linda tossed the last question around in her mind.

Amber halted, and Linda slid off the mare's back. Linda led her into her stall and untacked her. Amber wasn't sweaty, so Linda gave her a good brushing, then turned her out to graze with the other horses.

With a kick of her heels, the mare galloped across the pasture. Her cream-colored mane and tail flew behind her. She found a dusty spot and rolled around in it. Her long legs kicking in the air, Amber flopped from side to side. Then she scrambled to her feet and gave a satisfied shake. Dust flew everywhere.

Linda grinned. Sometimes she wondered why she even bothered brushing her.

As Linda walked back to the barn, she again thought about that one nagging question. Someone had deliberately let Amber out. Why?

Linda hung up her saddle and bridle. Then she closed the stall door and latched it. For a second, she stared at the new lock.

What if Page had told Mr. Greene that Amber could open stall doors? If he let Amber out, the mare would naturally look guilty. Which is exactly what happened.

Eager to ask Page if she *had* told Mr. Greene about Amber, Linda bolted from the barn and ran up the drive to the house. She dashed into the kitchen, where Luisa was fixing lunch.

"Hi, Luisa. Have you seen Page?" she asked.

"On the patio," Luisa replied. "How about having lunch out there?"

"Sounds good." Linda poured herself a glass of lemonade, then walked through the dining room to the patio. Page was stretched out in a lounge chair, sunning herself. She'd changed to shorts and a halter top.

Linda plopped down into a chair beside her. Page stared across the garden, ignoring her.

Linda tried to relax for a minute and enjoy the beauty of Doña's garden. The beavertail cactus and goldpoppy were blooming. The yuccas with their spiky leaves were just beginning to flower.

Then her gaze returned to her guest. Page's fingers gripped the arms of the lounge chair and there was a stony expression on her face. Linda knew she was still angry.

Somehow, she had to get her to listen.

"I've been doing some thinking about Sheik's disappearance," she began slowly.

Page didn't move or speak.

At least she didn't get up and leave, Linda thought. That was a good sign.

"And I want to prove that I didn't let your horse out, and Amber didn't, either," she continued.

She glanced over at Page. The other girl was frowning.

"First, I checked the latch in Amber's stall. There's no way she could have opened it. It must have been a person who did."

Linda paused and sipped her lemonade. When she

looked up, Page had stopped frowning and was watching her out of the corner of her eye.

"*I'd* never let a valuable horse like Sheik out," Linda went on. "Even if I were jealous. Besides, I love animals too much to do something that might hurt one."

Page's gaze dropped down, then over at Linda. "I know," she said quietly.

"You do? Then why'd you blame me?"

"I guess . . ." A tear slid down Page's cheek. She wiped at it, then struggled to clear her throat. "I guess because I was upset and mad about a lot of things and I took it out on everybody. Mostly you."

"Oh," Linda said, nodding. She was glad Page had sort of apologized for the way she'd acted.

"So who do you think did it?" Page asked.

Linda leaned toward her. "Mr. Greene," she whispered.

"Mr. Greene?" Page looked puzzled.

"Yes! He knew Sheik was at the ranch. And he really wanted to buy him, right?"

"Right."

"And you wouldn't sell, so he figured out another way to get him."

"He stole him!" Page said, sitting up straight in her chair.

"No." Linda waved away that idea. "Too risky. But

think how terrible Sheik will look if he's lost for several days. His coat will be sunburned. His mane and tail will be matted and his hooves chipped. You wouldn't be able to show him for a month."

Page nodded slowly, taking in everything Linda was saying.

"He'd look so terrible, you'd be glad to sell him," Linda added. "Except there's one hitch." She hesitated for a moment. "Why would Mr. Greene let Amber out, too? He would've had to know about Amber being able to open her door." She looked expectantly at Page. "Then he'd let both horses out, so it would look like Amber's fault."

Page thought for a minute. "You know," she said, "I did mention Amber. When I was telling Mr. Greene how Sheik almost jumped the fence."

"Then it really could be Mr. Greene!" Linda exclaimed.

Just then Luisa bustled onto the patio, carrying a tray. "Lunch," she said cheerfully.

"Great! I'm hungry." Linda helped the housekeeper put the dishes of food on the low glass table. There were bowls of cooked hamburger, grated cheese, shredded lettuce, tomato bits, a jar of hot sauce, a plate of taco shells, and a jug of lemonade.

"Doña will join you in a few minutes," Luisa said. "Can I get you girls anything else?"

"No thanks, this looks great." Linda and Page pulled their chairs up to the table. Luisa took the tray and left. "I hope you like tacos," Linda said.

She glanced over at her guest. Page's scowl had returned. Only this time it was more of a worried frown.

"What's wrong?" Linda asked.

"Everything." Page groaned. "So *what* if we figured out who did it and why. That still won't bring Sheik back."

Linda set down the taco she'd been making. "You're right. We've got to find him before something happens to him."

Page leaned forward in the lounge chair. Tears once again misted her eyes. "But how are we going to find him on this huge ranch? If he was nearby, your grandfather would have found him by now."

Linda bit her lip. She had to admit that Page was right. The ranch covered thousands of acres. It would take days of searching unless they had an idea which way the stallion had headed.

Suddenly, Linda remembered the deer tracks in the mud. "I know how we'll find him," she exclaimed. "By his hoofprints!"

5 ♦♦♦♦

"Hoofprints?" Page repeated. "How will they help us? There must be a million of them out there."

"But Sheik's are different from the other horses' prints." Linda leaped up excitedly from the table. "I noticed it the first day he was here. His hooves are real narrow and pointy."

"That's right!" Page's eyes grew wide. "We had him shod that way before we came here."

"All we need to do is find his trail and follow it. Come on!" Linda turned just as Doña stepped onto the patio.

"Hello, girls," Doña said with a smile. "I haven't seen you two all morning. Any luck in finding Sheik?"

"Uh . . ." Linda hesitated. Usually she told her grandmother everything. But what if the hoofprint idea was just a wild-goose chase?

"No sign of him yet," Page said quickly. "Did any of your neighbors see him?"

Doña shook her head, then smiled reassuringly at Page. "I hope you're not worrying too much."

"No. Linda's been cheering me up," Page said. To Linda's amazement, she even smiled.

"I'm not surprised," Doña said, smiling at her granddaughter. "That food looks delicious," she added as she crossed the patio and pulled up a chair next to Page.

Slowly, Linda sat down. She glanced meaningfully at Page.

The blond girl mouthed the words, "We'll look later." Then she reached for the hot sauce.

Linda finished making her taco. She could tell by the glint in Doña's dark eyes that her grandmother knew they were up to something.

"May we be excused?" Linda finally asked, after gulping down the last of her lunch.

Page put down her napkin and started to push back her chair.

Doña looked at Linda and Page curiously. "You girls are certainly in a hurry."

"We have to keep looking for Sheik," Page said.

"Well, good luck, and let me know as soon as the riders return."

The two girls stood up at the same time and bumped into each other. Page started giggling.

Waving goodbye to Doña, Linda showed Page the stone path behind the house. They raced around the carport and down the drive.

"Let's check Sheik's stall," Linda suggested. "We should be able to track him from there."

But the aisle in the barn had been swept clean.

"Too bad," Page said. "How about by the outside doors?"

"Good idea."

The dirt in the doorway was so full of hoofprints and bootprints, Linda couldn't tell one from the other.

"This is impossible." Page sighed.

Linda agreed, but she refused to give up. "I've got a plan. We'll fan out in a circle around the barn—you know, Page, like a search party."

She headed toward the field in front of the house. Page followed close behind. In the dirt by the gate, there were several clear prints. But none of them was Sheik's.

They looked along the fence. Nothing.

"I give up," Page said, collapsing in the shade of an orange tree.

"Not me." Squinting in the sun, Linda looked over

at her. "Come on. We've still got a lot of ground to cover."

Slowly, the blond girl got to her feet. "Let's face it," she grumbled. "Your hoofprint idea wasn't so hot. What if Sheik ran across the grass? We'd never see his tracks."

"There's *got* to be a sign of him somewhere," Linda insisted. "We can't give up. We haven't checked the drive yet."

"Wouldn't we have heard him going past the house?"

"In the middle of the night? I don't know about you, but I was pretty beat after the show."

"Yeah, me, too," Page admitted.

"Come on." Linda waved her ahead. "You take one side of the drive and I'll take the other."

Heads bent, the girls gradually paced up the drive and past the house. Linda concentrated on the dirt edge. She knew Sheik wouldn't stay on the hard gravel. And as Page said, they wouldn't be able to see any prints in the grass.

She was about to give up, when Page shouted.

Linda rushed over to Page and looked at where the other girl was pointing. There, in the soft dirt, was a single, narrow hoofprint.

"Is it Sheik's?" Page asked.

Linda nodded, then pointed. "Look. There's

another . . . and another. They lead to the road!''
She ran down the drive, Page following behind.

At the end of the driveway, the tracks turned right
and followed the main road. The girls traced them for
ten feet, then the trail vanished.

"Maybe he crossed the road," Linda suggested.
They searched and searched, but there was no further
sign of Sheik's hoofprints.

"And the ground's nice and soft," Page said.
"You'd think they'd be easy to spot."

"Let's go back to where we lost them," Linda said.

They crossed the road. Linda squatted down and
carefully looked at the tracks.

"I don't get it," she said. She pushed her hair
behind her ears. "They just disappear." She peered
more closely at the ground. "Wait a minute," she said
suddenly. "Look at this."

Page bent down. "It's a tire track. So what?"

"But it's from a truck that pulled off the road onto
the side," Linda explained. "Look at the zigzag
pattern in the tread."

She glanced up at Page. For a moment, they just
stared at each other.

"You mean somebody loaded him into a truck?"
Page finally asked. Her blue eyes were frightened.

"I don't know," Linda said, shaking her head. She
thought for a minute, then said, "If someone *did* load

Sheik into a truck, then that person's prints should be around here, too."

"Like this one!" Page exclaimed. She pointed to a spot by her foot. "It's not mine."

Linda stood up and set her boot beside the print. "Not mine, either. Too big. It looks like a man's cowboy boot."

"Mr. Greene's! Do you really think he could be a horse thief?" Page asked.

Linda shrugged her shoulders. "I don't know," she said.

Just then they heard the roar of a motor. Both girls hopped back from the road.

A second later, a jeep veered around the corner and skidded to a stop. Phil leaned toward them from the driver's seat.

"What are you two doing here?" he asked.

"We figured out what happened to Sheik!" Page exclaimed. "Mr. Greene stole him!"

For a second, Phil just looked at them with a puzzled expression on his face. Then he started to laugh. "Ralph Greene? Where'd you get a crazy idea like that?"

"It's not crazy," Linda said firmly.

She told Phil about Page meeting Ralph Greene at the show. Then Page explained Greene's interest in buying Sheik.

"And when I told him Sheik wasn't for sale, he still wanted to come out to the ranch," Page added.

Linda nodded. "Right. Plus, I remember Bronco and Mac saying Ralph Greene's been in on some shady deals," she said.

"And that's your proof? You guys have been out in the sun too long." Phil chuckled. "Climb in. I'll drive you back to the ranch."

"First, take a look at this," Linda insisted. She pointed to the hoofprints. "They're Sheik's. We tracked them from the drive to here. This is where they disappear."

"And look at this," Page broke in. "Tire tracks and a man's bootprint."

Phil raised an eyebrow. "That's it? A tire track along the road is hardly unusual. And how do you know that print is Sheik's?"

Linda told him.

"Sheik may have run this way," the trainer had to agree. "But I doubt if anyone took him."

He waved for them to get into the jeep. "I know you've both been worried and want to help. I didn't have any luck, either, but I'll bet when we get back to the ranch, the others will be there with Sheik."

"You're probably right," Page said. She climbed into the front of the jeep. "Come on, Linda. Let's go see if they've found him."

Linda hesitated. Phil may have laughed at her ideas, but she still thought there was something to them.

"Come on, Linda," Phil repeated. "Trying to blame Ralph Greene won't get Amber off the hook."

"But Amber's not guilty!" Linda protested, reluctantly climbing into the back of the jeep. Then Phil took off so fast, she didn't have a chance to say another word.

The jeep roared up the drive. Linda had to hold on to the side to keep from bouncing out. When they pulled up to the barn, the men were just riding in.

Page looked at them expectantly. "Any luck?" she asked in a hopeful voice.

Bronco shook his head wearily. The horses were covered with dust. Linda knew they must have covered a lot of ground.

"Oh, no!" Page cried.

"It seems like we searched everywhere," Bob said as he jumped down from Rocket.

Bronco dismounted more slowly. "I'm sorry, Page," he said. "But we'll look again tomorrow. One of the ranch hands picked up a trail when he was out checking the herd."

For once, Page didn't say anything. She just sat in the jeep, staring down at her lap.

Linda stood up in the back of the jeep. "We found a trail, too!"

"Where?"

"Going down the drive to the main road."

Bronco looked puzzled. "I figured if he went that way, someone would have spotted him."

"Doña phoned all the neighbors," Linda said. "No luck there."

"The girls have this crazy idea that Sheik was stolen," Phil said, grinning.

"What!" Bob laughed. "I'll bet that was Linda's idea."

Linda jumped from the back of the jeep. "You can laugh all you want, but when you see the evidence you won't think it's so funny," she said to her brother.

Bob stifled a grin.

Bronco held up his hand. "Hold it a minute. Let's hear what Linda and Page have to say."

Linda started to blurt out all they'd discovered. Then she bit her lip. What if Bronco and Mac laughed, too? But she trusted them. And she had to tell them what she and Page had found. Just in case Sheik *had* been stolen.

Mac and Bronco listened carefully while she and Page told the whole story.

When they'd finished, Bob shook his head doubtfully. "I don't know. It doesn't make sense."

Linda ignored him. "What do you think?" she asked, looking back and forth at Mac and Bronco.

"Well, I doubt Sheik was stolen," Bronco said. "At least, not by Ralph Greene. He's not one of my favorite people, but he's no horse thief."

Mac dismounted and slapped the dust from his chaps. "Bronco's right. Ralph may have sold a lame horse or two, but he's never stolen one."

"Besides," Bronco added, "registered Arabians have a brand. Like our cattle. Except they have big numbers tattooed on their necks."

"Of course!" Phil cut in as he climbed out of the jeep. "Sheik's is zero-zero-eight-four-four-two-nine. So unless someone stole his papers, too, he'd be worthless. They couldn't show him, sell him, or anything."

"And the papers are in my safe," Bronco said. "Right where your father put them, Page."

Page was still slumped in the front seat of the jeep. "Oh" was all she said.

"But what about the hoofprints?" Linda asked. "I know they're Sheik's."

Phil slapped the hood of the jeep. "I know where they came from. After the show I walked Sheik along the drive. He needed cooling off."

"There you go," Mac said. "Case closed." He winked at Linda, then headed toward the barn.

Bronco smiled reassuringly at the two girls. "We'll find Sheik first thing in the morning," he said. He arched his back and groaned. "Now I need a hot shower and some of Luisa's lemonade."

He turned and started for the barn, his horse, Colonel, following behind him.

Page stepped slowly from the jeep.

"Maybe something cold to drink would cheer you up," Phil said to her.

"I guess," she agreed sadly. "Are you coming, Linda?"

"In a minute." Linda ran to catch up with Bronco. She fell into step beside him. "Where did the ranch hand find the trail?"

"Jim found it out on the mesa," Bronco said as he halted Colonel inside the barn. Linda held the horse's reins while Bronco undid the girth.

"The mesa!" she echoed. "How did Sheik get way out there?"

"We don't know for sure if it is his trail," Bronco said as he slid the saddle from Colonel's back. "It could have been a cow wandering from the herd. The ground was so hard, we couldn't tell what kind of animal it was." He carried the saddle into the tack room.

Linda got to work sponging off Colonel's dusty back. A moment later, Bronco returned with a halter. "Where were the tracks headed?" Linda asked him.

Bronco was silent for a minute. "Toward Rattlesnake Gulch," he said finally.

Linda's heart sank.

Rattlesnake Gulch was a long ravine. The sides were dangerously steep and rocky, and the bottom was bone dry. Nothing lived there except prickly cactus, lizards, and rattlesnakes. It would be easy for a pampered horse like Sheik, who wasn't a range horse, to get hurt there.

"Maybe he was smart enough to stay away," Linda said hopefully.

"I don't know." Bronco shook his head, a grim set to his jaw. "Jim followed the trail to the edge of the gulch, and whatever made those tracks seemed to disappear right over the side."

6 ♦♦♦♦

"You mean Sheik could be trapped down there!" Linda cried.

"We just don't know," Bronco said. "There was a lot of broken rock and a slide mark in the dirt. It could have been another animal. Jim climbed halfway down the gulch, but it got too steep. And we were all too tired to risk climbing down on ropes. We'll do it tomorrow."

"Why don't we go now?"

Bronco shook his head. "By the time we got to the gulch, it would be dark."

"Oh, right. I forgot about that." Linda wrinkled her nose. "Anyway, I wouldn't want to climb into that gulch at night. All those rattlesnakes just waiting for you."

Bronco chuckled. "Has Mac been telling you his rattlesnake stories again?"

"Just the one about the snake that bit his boot. Is it true?"

"It's true. But don't believe the rumors that there are thousands of rattlers down there. The real reason it's called Rattlesnake Gulch is because it's so long and winding."

"That makes sense," Linda muttered, feeling sort of silly for believing Mac's tall tales. And she'd only seen a rattler once.

"But suppose Sheik *is* down there," Linda continued. "What could happen to him?"

"The biggest problem with the gulch is its steep sides," Bronco said over his shoulder, as he led Colonel into his stall. "If an animal falls into the gulch, it might take him days to climb out."

A knot of fear formed in Linda's stomach. "How long could Sheik survive without water?"

"I don't know. It depends on whether he's hurt or not."

Bronco slipped the halter off Colonel, threw him some hay, then closed the door and turned to Linda.

"It'll probably take us all morning to search the length of Rattlesnake Gulch," he said.

"And this time I'm coming with you!" Linda said firmly to her grandfather.

Bronco chuckled as he strode from the barn. Linda

went into the tack room to wipe off Amber's bit. She wanted everything ready so tomorrow she could saddle up quickly.

At six A.M. the Southern California sun was bright as it rose over the hills.

Everyone had gathered in the kitchen at daybreak to discuss the search. Now Linda, Bob, and Mac were outside the barn, mounted on their horses. Phil and Bronco were loading up the jeep.

Page was still asleep. Bronco had decided not to take her to Rattlesnake Gulch. He knew she wasn't used to rough range-riding, and he didn't want her to be upset if they failed to find Sheik.

"Mac, Bob, Linda—I'd like you three to ride to the north end of the gulch," Bronco said from the driver's seat of the jeep. "Phil and I will drive to the southern end. Both groups will work their way to the middle. Remember, Sheik could be anywhere in the gulch."

As she listened, Linda stroked Amber's neck. The mare was as excited as her rider. They both loved adventure, but something more was at stake. They *had* to find Sheik!

"Is that clear?" Bronco finished. They all nodded. "Then let's go," he said.

The jeep sped along the drive.

Mac reined his horse, Buck, around and headed east past the big corral. Linda followed at a slow jog. Bob gave Rocket a kick, and cantered past the other two horses.

Mac shook his head at Bob and Rocket. "At that rate, those two will be tired out before we get there."

Linda nodded in agreement. Amber pranced sideways. The mare wanted to take off after Rocket, but Linda held her back.

"Easy, girl," she crooned. "We've got a long ride ahead of us."

They rode steadily for an hour. As the horses jogged east, the pastureland turned into rocky brown mesa. Clumps of sagebrush and patches of wildflowers dotted the flat land. Finally, Mac pointed to a mound of rocks in the distance.

"There's the beginning of the gulch," he said. "It's about a mile away."

"Meet you there!" Linda called over her shoulder to Bob and Mac. Amber had been dying to run all morning. Linda pressed her heels in the mare's side, and they shot forward.

Amber sensed her rider's excitement. The palomino's stride lengthened. The warm wind whistled across Linda's cheeks.

Suddenly, a whoop came from behind them.

Surprised, Linda glanced over her shoulder. Bob and Rocket were thundering toward them. "Race you!" Bob shouted as he caught up to them.

Linda flattened down on Amber's neck. "Okay, girl," she whispered in Amber's ear. "Let's go!"

The mare flicked her ears at the sound of her rider's voice. Instantly, she surged forward, her hooves pounding the dry ground like drumbeats. They galloped faster and faster. Linda laughed out loud. It felt as if they were flying!

She turned her head and saw Bob and Rocket falling behind. Her brother was scowling.

Linda pulled gently on the reins and sat deeper in the saddle. Amber slowed to a canter.

"We did it! We beat Bob!" Linda told her. They cantered to a clump of rocks near the deep ravine. When Amber saw the jagged edge, she slid to a halt. Nervously, she backed up several steps.

Linda soothed her with a pat on the neck. Then she stood in the stirrups and peered over the edge of the gulch. Sharp rocks jutted from the steep sides. Branches and logs, washed from flash floods, hid the bottom.

Bob trotted up beside Linda. "Show-off," he said good-naturedly. "But just wait, one of these days,

Rocket and I will beat you." Then he stared into the gulch and gave a low whistle. "Looks pretty rough, doesn't it?"

Linda nodded. "I almost hope Sheik isn't down there," she said.

Just then, Mac cantered past them. Linda and Bob turned their horses and followed him. He was heading south, winding his way along the edge of the gulch.

"About a mile from here is where Jim saw the tracks," he told them when they'd caught up. "So keep your eyes open."

For fifteen minutes, the three riders followed the twists and turns of the ravine. Linda watched carefully for signs of the stallion. But the area seemed empty of life.

Finally, Bob halted Rocket. "Here's the pile of stones Jim left as a marker," he said, dismounting. He tied Rocket to a tree.

Linda was about to jump off Amber, when the mare raised her head in alarm and nickered loudly.

"It could be that she hears Sheik," Mac said. He got off Buck and tied him to another tree, near Rocket. "That horse definitely has a sixth sense."

Linda dismounted and tied Amber next to Buck. Restlessly, the mare pawed the ground.

Linda gave the reins a tug to make sure the knot was secure. Then she joined Mac and Bob.

"I'll go first," Bob said. He looped a rope around his waist, then tied it to a tree trunk. After making sure it was tight enough, he began climbing down the wall of rock.

"Okay, Linda, you follow him," Mac said. He helped her secure a rope around her waist. "Take it slow," he cautioned.

With one hand on the rope, Linda began to lower herself over the edge.

At first the jutting rocks were like steps. Then they grew steeper. The soles of her cowboy boots were slick, and she had trouble getting a foothold.

Suddenly, her left foot slipped out from under her.

"Oh!" she cried, grabbing for the rope with her other hand.

"Are you all right?" Mac called down to her.

"I can't find a good toehold!" she hollered.

"I see a ledge to your left. Swing your foot onto it."

Linda bent her leg, searching for the ledge. When she found it, she pulled herself onto it.

For a second she hugged the rock, breathing hard.

"Take it a little slower!" Bob called up to her.

Linda nodded, then leaned back to see where she could go. On the other side of the ledge, a huge trapped log jutted into the air from the bottom of the gulch.

Taking tiny steps, Linda inched toward it. Her stomach was pressed flat against the wall of rock, and her fingers were wedged in a crack above her head.

She'd almost reached the log, when she felt something slither over her hand. She froze. Her heart began thumping wildly.

"Please don't let it be a snake," she whispered.

Slowly, she raised her eyes. A tiny lizard stared back at her. It flicked its tongue, then scurried away.

Linda groaned in relief.

"You coming?" Bob called.

Linda nodded, then grabbed a root and stepped from her perch onto the log. She straddled it, trying to catch her breath.

"I'm glad that's over with!" she said, wiping the sweat from her brow. Then she realized how scared she must sound. And she didn't want Bob to think a little lizard had frightened her.

"That was incredible!" she added with a laugh.

Bob raised his eyebrows. "Incredible?" he said. "You look a little white in the face to me."

The sound of falling rock made them look up. Hand over hand, Mac was lowering himself down the side. He jumped the last five feet.

"You must think we're mountain goats," he grumbled to Bob. "Some route you picked!"

Linda inched down the log. Mac uncapped his canteen, and they all took a drink. Then they headed off along the gulch floor.

Soon they came to a wider area. Catclaw and creosote bush grew thick in the sandy bottom. Linda, Bob, and Mac were walking along a narrow path, when they heard a loud snort.

The three of them stopped dead.

Leaves rustled. Then a branch snapped.

"Do you think it's Sheik?" Linda whispered.

Mac put his finger to his lips. He waved for Linda and Bob to follow. Silently, they wound their way through the bushes. Then they saw it.

Fifteen feet in front of them stood a whiteface cow. She snorted but didn't run away.

"What's she doing down here?" Bob asked in a low voice.

Mac grinned and pointed to a bush by the cow's feet. Curled under it lay a spotted calf. Its big brown eyes stared up at them.

"Do you think it's hurt?" Linda asked.

At the sound of her voice, the cow mooed. The calf scrambled to its feet and began to butt its mother's side, trying to nurse.

Bob laughed. "It seems to be okay."

"Well, now we know whose tracks Jim saw," Linda said.

"I'll bet the calf fell into the gulch, and the cow went after it," Mac said. "Usually, the cattle stay away from here."

"How are we going to get them out?" Linda asked.

Mac pointed down the ravine. "We're near the break in the walls. We'll drive them toward it, then they should be able to climb out."

He took off his cowboy hat and waved it in the air. With a snort, the cow turned and ambled away from them. The calf trotted after her.

They walked about fifty feet, then Mac pointed to the side of the gulch. Here it sloped up gently, and Linda could see the top. It would be an easy climb for the cow and her calf.

Mac and Bob drove the cow upward. She lunged up the bank. The calf tried to scramble after her, but it fell to its knees. Quickly, Mac picked up the calf. He cradled its neck with one arm and wrapped the other around its rump.

Linda and Bob hurried up to the top of the gulch. They waved their arms at the cow to keep her from going after Mac and her calf. The ranch foreman got his balance and, with a grunt, climbed the last few feet out of the gulch.

When he laid the calf on the ground, it leaped up and galloped to its mother's side. The white tuft on the end of its tail swished happily.

Without a backward glance, mother and baby took off across the mesa.

Mac slapped the dirt from his pants and shirt. "I'm glad that's done. Now let's get back to the horses."

When Amber saw Linda, she whinnied a greeting. Linda opened her saddlebag and passed out apples and granola bars. Then she gave Amber her treat. The mare took the apple gently from Linda's palm.

They mounted and continued along the gulch for another hour. Nothing stirred in the deep ravine, and there were no more tracks. Linda was getting discouraged.

"Why don't we stop here and wait for Phil and Bronco," Mac suggested. "It looks cool." He nodded toward a grove of mesquite trees.

Just then, they heard the roar of the jeep behind them. Surprised by the noise, Amber wheeled around. Linda grabbed the saddle horn to steady herself.

The jeep's brakes squealed as it came to an abrupt stop. Phil jumped out, a worried frown on his face. "Is Page with you?" he asked anxiously.

All three riders shook their heads.

"What's the matter?" Linda asked.

Phil ran his fingers through his hair. "Doña just called on the CB radio," he told her. "It seems Sheik isn't the only one who's disappeared. Now Page is missing, too!"

7 ◆◆◆◆

"Now, take it easy, Phil," Bronco said, climbing out of the jeep. "All Doña said was that Page has been gone since this morning."

"You're right. I'm sorry," the trainer said. "It's just that I'm responsible for her. I was hoping she'd joined up with you guys. When I saw she wasn't with you, I kind of panicked."

"She didn't know we were going to search Rattlesnake Gulch," Bob pointed out.

"Where would she go?" Linda asked Bronco.

"I don't know," he replied. "Doña said Page saddled up one of the ranch horses and took off shortly after we did."

"Well-l-l," Mac drawled. "I guess we'd better go back and find out where she's gone."

"Actually, she's done this before," Phil said. "At the auction where we bought Sheik, she disappeared for a few hours. Nathan says she does it to get attention."

"We'd still better head back," Bronco said. He turned to Linda, Bob, and Mac. "I guess you three didn't have any luck finding Sheik," he said.

"All we found was a cow and her calf," Linda said. "The cow's tracks were the ones Jim saw."

Bronco nodded. Then he reached into the back seat of the jeep, opened a cooler, and pulled out a handful of foil-wrapped sandwiches. "Here, eat while you ride," he said, handing one to Bob.

He passed out the rest, then got out some cans of juice. Linda knotted her reins together, then looped them over the saddle horn so she could use her hands to eat.

"Now, don't you move," she warned Amber. "Or I'll spill my drink all over your mane."

Phil and Bronco climbed back into the jeep, and with a wave, they roared ahead of the riders and disappeared over the horizon.

Mac, Bob, and Linda turned their horses and began the trip home, walking slowly so they could eat.

"Some lunch," Bob grumbled as he finished his sandwich. "Phil and Bronco will probably eat all the cake Luisa packed."

"I doubt it," Linda said. "I think Phil's too worried about Page to eat."

Tipping back his head, Bob drained his drink. "One thing *I'm* not worried about is Page," he said, crushing the can in his hand. "Somehow I've got the feeling that whatever Page is up to, she can take care of herself."

"I don't know about that," Linda said. "She really is upset about Sheik. And she doesn't know her way around the ranch."

Bob laughed. "I can just see her now, riding one of our old cow ponies in her tight britches and high black boots."

"You're not being fair," Linda said after a minute. "I think Page is just trying too hard to impress everybody."

"So when did you get to be her best friend?" Bob said teasingly. "I thought she accused you of letting Sheik out."

"She was just upset." Linda crumpled up the piece of foil and stuck it, along with her empty juice can, in her saddlebag.

"I'm going to ride on ahead, since I've finished eating," she told Mac and her brother. "See you at the house."

Linda urged Amber into a trot, then relaxed back in

the saddle. Her body rocked with the rhythm of the easy gait as she left Bob and Mac behind.

At the bottom of a grassy hill, Amber sensed that they were almost home. She broke into a canter and leaped to the top of the hill.

"Whoa," Linda said. The mare halted. Linda rested her hands on the saddle horn. Rancho del Sol stretched before her like a picture.

For a moment, she wondered what it would be like to live in the city, like Page. Linda knew she'd hate it. She'd miss everything about the ranch—even the hard work.

"Come on, girl, let's go home," Linda said. And with no further coaxing, Amber plunged down the hill and galloped toward the ranch.

All of a sudden, a jackrabbit dashed from a clump of grass and ran straight for them. Linda pulled on the reins, but Amber was quicker. The mare swerved sharply to miss the darting rabbit. Then she wheeled on her hind legs and, with her head low, started after it.

Laughing, Linda hung on to the saddle horn. Amber must have thought she was a cow pony!

The mare twisted and turned after the rabbit. Linda's body jerked back and forth as it followed the mare's movements. Finally, the rabbit jumped a pile of rocks and ducked down a hole. Amber slid to a halt and stared at the spot where the rabbit had disappeared.

"Whew!" Linda gasped. "That was some ride. Wait till Bob hears you've decided to be a cow pony, too!"

Linda knew her brother would have been mad if he'd been there to see Amber. He'd been training Rocket for a month to do the exact same thing Amber had just done naturally.

"Someday, we'll have to practice with a real cow," Linda told the mare as she turned Amber back toward the ranch.

An hour later, the mare was untacked, cooled down, and contentedly munching hay in her stall. The others had already arrived back at the ranch and had gone up to the house for a cool drink.

Linda swung her saddle off the stall door. As she did, she suddenly spotted a piece of folded-up paper tucked into a crack in the door.

She set the saddle on the floor. Then she plucked the paper from the door. She unfolded the paper and read:

Dear Linda,

You were right about Sheik. Meet me at Melton's Gas Station.

Quickly, Linda reread the note. She knew Page meant that Linda was right about Sheik having been stolen. But how did Melton's Gas Station tie in with the theft?

Linda refolded the note and stuck it in her pocket. Amber stopped chewing and stared at her. A clump of hay hung from the side of Amber's mouth.

Linda couldn't help laughing. Then she became serious. She leaned against the stall door and thought about what she should do.

She had to meet Page at Melton's. But should she tell anyone why she was going?

No. They'd figure Page was just looking for attention again. And maybe that's all it was. But Linda had to find out.

She looked at Amber, wondering if the horse would be too tired for another ride after being out all morning. But the gas station was only on the outskirts of town, so it wasn't a long trip.

Then Amber stopped eating. She stuck her nose in Linda's face and blew softly on her cheek.

"All right, girl." Linda scratched her under the silky mane. "You can go. I just thought you might be too tired."

Quickly, she saddled the palomino. Then she wrote a message on the back of Page's note.

Rode to Melton's Gas Station. Be back by dinner.

Linda

She tacked her note on the barn bulletin board, then mounted Amber.

They took a back trail toward Lockwood. When they got to the gas station, Linda turned Amber off the path. Carefully she steered the mare past old junked cars and smelly tires. As she neared the building, she heard someone call her name.

"Over here!" Page jumped up and waved her arms at Linda. She'd been sitting under a Joshua tree. A bay horse was grazing next to her. It was Smokey Joe, one of the ranch's cow ponies.

Smokey Joe raised his head when he saw Amber and gave a nicker of greeting.

The mare trotted over to him.

"Where have you been!" Page cried. Her eyes glowed with excitement as she grabbed hold of Amber's reins. "It seems like I've been sitting here all day!" she said. "Wait till you hear my news. I've got proof that Sheik *was* stolen. Which means he's not lost on the ranch . . ."

"Hold on!" Linda said, but Page only talked faster.

"You just need to talk to Jack, the guy who was working at the gas station last night. He'll tell you . . ."

"Page!" Linda shouted. She had spoken so loudly she startled Amber.

Page stopped talking and blinked in surprise. "What?" she finally said.

Linda's eyes sparkled with excitement as she slid off Amber and led her under the tree. "Now, slow down and start at the beginning!" she said.

"Okay." Page took a deep breath. "You remember the hoofprints and the bootprint by the main road? And remember how everyone laughed at us when we said they proved Sheik was stolen?"

Linda nodded quickly.

"And Phil said that he'd walked Sheik down there after the show?"

"Right."

"Well, that bootprint couldn't have been Phil's!" Page leaned forward and clutched Linda's arm. "You told me it was made by a cowboy boot. But Phil doesn't *have* any cowboy boots. He only wears English riding boots!"

Linda thought for a minute. Then she said, "You're right. The prints would look different."

Page nodded. "I checked just to be sure. I took one of Phil's boots and set it by the print. It wasn't even close."

Linda took a deep breath.

"And besides that," Page continued, "Phil would never walk Sheik along the road. It's too dangerous! And you know Phil, he'd never do anything to hurt a horse."

Slowly, Linda let out her breath. "Which means . . ."

". . . that Sheik *was* stolen," Page finished for her. "You were right all along!"

"I don't get it," Linda said, plopping down on the grass. "Why would Phil say he walked Sheik along the road when he didn't?"

Page sat next to her. "I think he just said that to try to make me feel better," she replied. "He probably thought I'd be twice as upset if I was convinced that Sheik had been stolen."

"That makes sense," Linda said, nodding.

"But I haven't told you about the tire tracks yet!" Page said.

Linda looked at her. Then her eyes lit up.

"That's right!" she said excitedly. "If someone did take Sheik they'd have to haul him past this gas station—*if* they were heading toward Lockwood."

Page jumped up. "That's why I came here. I found out that the station was open late Saturday night, and I thought someone might have noticed a truck and trailer or a van."

"And did anyone?"

"Yes! Jack, one of the attendants, was filling somebody's car at about one o'clock, when a pickup pulling a trailer went down the road." She jumped up. "And do you know why he noticed it?"

Linda shook her head, her eyes fixed on Page's face.

"Because the horse inside the trailer was kicking so hard, Jack thought he'd bust right through the side!"

"Wow! That definitely sounds like Sheik!"

Page grinned proudly at Linda. Then her smile faded. "But if I'm right, it means I may never see Sheik again," she said.

"We'll get him back." Linda scrambled to her feet. "Maybe Jack remembers something else. I'll go ask him."

"Good idea," Page agreed. "I'll watch the horses."

Jack, a young man in his late teens, was pumping gas into an old, beat-up sedan. Linda walked across the hot asphalt toward him.

"I hear you're looking for a lost horse," Jack said as he stuck the nozzle back into the gas pump.

"That's right. And we think he might have been in that trailer you saw. Do you remember what the pickup pulling it looked like?"

He thought for a minute. "Sure," he said finally. "It was bright blue with a gold stripe along the side. I remember because the trailer was painted to match."

"How about the license plate number?"

"Sorry, I didn't notice it," replied Jack.

"Well, which way were they going?"

"Let's see. North. Yeah, it was heading north toward town."

"Thanks, Jack," Linda said. She ran back to Page and the horses.

"What did he say?" Page wanted to know.

"The pickup was blue, with a gold stripe down the side," Linda told her. "Now I think it's time we called Bronco and told him." She dug in her pockets. "Oh, no! I don't have any money."

"No problem." Page pulled a wallet from her saddlebag and handed Linda a fistful of coins. Linda raced into the gas station office to use the pay phone. She dialed quickly. The phone at the ranch rang once, twice, three times.

"Come on . . . Somebody answer!" Linda said impatiently. She hopped from foot to foot. She was sure that when Bronco heard the latest news, he'd call the police. And the sooner, the better!

Suddenly, she saw Page waving frantically in front of the window, trying to get her attention.

Linda stood on tiptoe to see what Page was pointing at.

Then she gasped.

It was the blue pickup!

8 ♦♦♦♦

Linda dropped the receiver and left it dangling.

"Talk about luck!" she whispered to herself. She dashed to the door to get a better look. At the same time, Page ran into the office so fast she crashed right into Linda. Linda grabbed Page's hand and pulled her to the window.

"I wish we could see inside the cab!" Linda whispered in Page's ear.

Page peered through the window. "I think I see two men."

"Is one of them Ralph Greene?"

"I can't tell. Let me get closer." Page stepped toward the doorway. Linda yanked her back.

"They might recognize you!" she said. She bit her lip and thought for a minute. "I have an idea. Follow me."

Bending low, the two girls scurried out the door and across the asphalt. They hunched down behind an old car. Heads together, they peered around a rusty bumper.

"Why are we over here if we're trying to see who's in the truck?" Page asked, puzzled.

"Shhh!" Linda put a finger to her lips. "We're going to check the tires."

"Tires?"

Linda nodded. "Remember? The tire prints by the side of the road had that funny zigzag in them. There could be thousands of blue pickups out there. But there's not much chance of their having the same kind of tires!"

"Oh, yeah!" Page said slowly. "All we need to do is check to see if these match the ones we saw on the main road." She stood up.

Linda grabbed her arm and pulled her down. "We can't go running over there. They'll spot us in the rearview mirror."

"But I can't see the tires from here."

"If I stoop real low and stay dead center, they shouldn't be able to see me."

"Okay," Page said. "I'll be your lookout."

Linda set her cowboy hat on the ground. Then she dashed to the back of the truck. Hanging on to the rear bumper, she squatted down. She ran her finger along the deep grooves of a tire—it had a zigzag tread! She noted the license plate number, then scurried back to Page.

"SWH one-five-nine," she repeated. "Remember that."

"I'll remember," Page said. Then she clutched Linda's arm, squeezing it tightly. "They're leaving!" she said. "We can't let them get away."

Linda stood up, pulling Page with her. "Come on. Let's follow as far as we can on horseback. At least we can find out which way they go, then we'll call Bronco."

They kept their eyes on the truck as it pulled into the main road. Then they raced to the other side of the station and the horses.

Linda grabbed the saddle horn and vaulted onto Amber's back. She grasped the reins and clucked. Amber sprang forward so fast she had to hold on to her hat to keep it from flying off. As they got closer to the road, Linda looked back for Page.

The blond girl was still under the Joshua tree. She was hanging on to her horse's mane, one foot on the ground, the other halfway into the stirrup. Smokey Joe danced sideways, afraid Amber was leaving him.

Quickly, Linda returned to Page's side.

"Whoa!" Linda said. Smokey Joe stood still just long enough for Page to swing onto his back.

The girls reined their horses around, and rode off after the truck.

The truck had gone north toward Lockwood. Linda knew they'd be able to ride the horses along the wide, grassy roadside for about a quarter of a mile. Then they'd have to turn onto the trail.

Though they galloped a safe distance behind, Linda was able to keep the truck in sight. Then its rear signal flickered. The truck slowed down and made a right turn onto a dirt road.

Linda tugged on the reins, and Amber dropped down to a trot. When they reached the turnoff, she brought the mare to a stop. Smokey Joe came to a halt beside them.

"Why are we stopping?" Page asked.

"Because the truck turned in here," Linda explained.

"We don't want to lose them. Come on!"

Linda reached for Smokey Joe's reins to stop Page. "But I know where that road leads. And it doesn't go anywhere."

"It has to go somewhere," Page protested.

"Just to a ghost town," Linda said. "The state bought it. They're going to fix it up and make it into a park."

"But that's a perfect hideout!" Page exclaimed. "Who'd ever think of looking for a stolen horse in a ghost town?" She reined Smokey Joe around. "You're right, we don't need to go any farther. Let's call the police." She kicked the gelding. Reluctantly, he trotted a few steps away from Amber, back the way they'd come. "Are you coming?" Page called to Linda.

Linda twisted around in the saddle. "I don't know about calling the police, Page. I mean, we still don't have any real proof that Sheik's at the ghost town. What if the police go roaring in after whoever's in the pickup and find out they're park rangers or something?"

"Good point," Page said, reining her horse around again. "Then the only thing to do is follow the truck and find out if Sheik's there."

"That could be dangerous," Linda said in a low voice.

For a second they just looked at each other, trying to decide what to do. Several cars roared by. One honked its horn, and Amber danced sideways. With a shake of her head, the mare pulled the reins through Linda's fingers. Then she took off down the dirt road at a fast trot.

"Hey!" Linda sputtered, trying to grab the dangling reins.

Grinning, Page cantered up beside her.

"I think Amber made the decision for us!" she

said. "Now, let's go find Sheik!" She slapped the end of the reins against Smokey Joe's shoulder, and with a loud "yee-ya" passed Linda and Amber.

Linda had to laugh. Page was wearing her tight britches and English boots, but she was acting like a cowboy. And for the first time, she was really riding!

Even Smokey Joe was excited. He pulled in front of Amber, his hooves flinging dust into the air. Amber trotted after him so fast that Linda had to post to keep her balance. As they rounded a bend, she caught sight of the ghost town.

Then it hit her. They couldn't go charging down the road like the cavalry. The thieves—if they were there—would see them!

"Slow down!" she called to Page.

Page glanced over her shoulder. Then she laughed, leaned forward, and yelled at Smokey Joe to go faster.

"Oh, no," Linda groaned. "She thinks we're racing!"

She had to stop Page before whoever was in the pickup saw her gallop into town!

Bending low on Amber's neck, Linda urged the mare to go faster. Amber shot forward, her silky mane whipping back and forth.

Dust flew into Linda's face, stinging her eyes. She

coughed and gritted her teeth. She had to catch up to them!

Page kept kicking Smokey Joe, urging him to go faster. But he was no match for Amber.

With a burst of speed, the sleek palomino caught up with him.

"Page!" Linda hollered. "Stop!"

Page looked over her shoulder, and when she saw the expression on Linda's face, she sat back in the saddle. Smokey Joe slid to a halt.

Linda reined Amber in.

"We have to do this quietly, without being seen," she explained as Amber reared up. "Follow me. I know another way into the town."

She motioned toward the right. Leaving the road, the two horses cantered up a hill. Then Linda led them down the other side to a rocky path.

"This will take us behind the old saloon. My friend Kathy and I used to come here a lot. There's a hitching post we can tie the horses to."

Minutes later, she pointed to a faded wooden building. The back door sagged on its hinges. Part of the roof had blown away.

"That's the old saloon," Linda said.

"It doesn't look much like a saloon," Page said as she dismounted.

Linda laughed. "That's because you're used to the fancy ones they show in old movies. This is what they really were like."

She slid off Amber and looped her reins around the hitching post. Page did the same.

"Better check your knot," Linda cautioned. "You don't want Smokey Joe to get loose."

Page yanked on the reins, then nodded.

"This way," Linda whispered. She pushed open the back door slowly, trying to keep it from groaning and creaking. Then she slid through the narrow opening.

It was pitch black inside.

Linda waited a second to let her eyes adjust to the dark. They were in the storeroom. Last year, she and Kathy had explored it from top to bottom hunting for old bottles and coins.

"Follow me," she whispered to Page. Stepping carefully, Linda moved toward a crack of light that she knew came from the door that led into the saloon. She opened the door and peered through. "All clear," she whispered.

Linda opened the door wider, and she and Page crept into the saloon.

"Wow," Page murmured behind her. "This place is amazing."

Like the outside of the building, the inside was

weathered and gray. Cobwebs hung from the ceiling. Mice and birds had littered the floor with grass and seeds.

But the old bar was still standing, just as if it were waiting for customers.

Linda walked to the swinging front doors. One sagged on its hinges. She peered over it, then waved to Page to join her.

"There's the blue pickup." Linda pointed across the street to the general store.

Then they both saw the trailer. It was parked by the side of the store. "That means Sheik *must* be here!" Page exclaimed.

"Shhh!" Linda cautioned.

"Where do you think they're hiding him?"

"The best place would be the old livery stable," replied Linda.

"Can we get to it without being seen?"

Linda nodded. "I think so. We'll sneak behind the buildings. Come on."

They went out through the back of the saloon. When Amber saw Linda, her ears flicked forward. Linda put a finger to her lips, signaling the mare to be quiet.

Checking to make sure no one was around, the girls dashed across the alley and hid behind an old shack.

"It's the next building down," Linda said.

She peered around the corner, then sprinted for the stable. Page darted after her.

"We made it!" Page said, catching her breath.

"Now we just have to get inside." Linda stepped away from the wall. About halfway down, a board had been knocked out. It left a space big enough for them to squeeze through.

When they'd climbed inside, Page grabbed hold of Linda's arm to make sure she was still there.

"I can't see anything!" she whispered, sounding frightened.

"Me, neither," Linda said. "Give your eyes a second to get used to the dark."

After a few minutes, Linda was able to make out their surroundings. They were standing on a dirt floor. A pile of rusty cans and rotting garbage was heaped in one corner. A mound of moldy hay was stacked up against the wall. A wooden ladder led to an opening in the plank ceiling. Probably a hay loft, thought Linda.

The stable opened up into a larger area with a high roof. Several stalls jutted from each side.

"It smells like rotting hay in here," Page said, wrinkling her nose.

Just then, a low nicker came from a dark corner.

Page clutched Linda's arm.

The girls tiptoed past the stack of hay and walked toward the stalls. Standing inside the first stall was a horse.

Page cried out before Linda could stop her, "Sheik!"

The girls rushed up to the horse. Sticking his head out over the door, the animal tossed his black mane.

Page stepped backward, a puzzled expression in her blue eyes. "That's not him!"

Linda frowned and looked over the side of the stall. It was an Arabian, all right. But this horse was all black, from his mane to his tail.

And yet, there was something familiar about him. The horse in the stall had the same perfectly arched neck and beautiful head. Linda held up the palm of her hand. The horse nuzzled it just as Sheik used to.

Linda studied the horse carefully. Didn't his cowlick swirl just the way Sheik's had? Or was it just her imagination?

And Linda was curious about the stallion's blue-black coat. It was darker than any she'd ever seen. She lightly brushed her fingers across his nose. A streak of black marked the inside of her hand.

"Page, look!" she whispered, holding out her

smudged fingers. "I think this horse has been dyed!" Page ran her own hand across the horse's back, and black colored her palm.

"You're right. I'll bet this *is* Sheik! But there's only one way to prove it."

She entered the stall and flipped the horse's long mane to the other side of his neck. "There it is!" she said, grinning broadly. "Sheik's tattoo—zero-zero-eight-four-four-two-nine."

She gave the stallion a hug. "If we can only get this gunk out of his coat."

"First we have to get him back to the ranch," Linda added in a serious voice. "There must be a halter somewhere."

She began to hunt around the dark barn.

Page stroked Sheik's neck. "You know, Linda," she said. "I don't get it. Your grandfather told us that Sheik would be worthless without his registration papers."

"I know," Linda answered from a dusty corner. She'd found an old, rusty tack box. Inside were a halter and a lead line. She pulled them out and handed them to Page.

"Then why would someone steal him? They couldn't sell him or show him."

"I don't know," Linda murmured, only half listening. She was looking at a piece of paper that had been hidden under the halter. She pulled out the paper and held it up to a ray of light.

"Oh, no!" she gasped, after she'd read what was written on it. "Sheik is being shipped out of the country!"

9 ♦♦♦♦

"What!" Page quickly snapped the lead line onto Sheik's halter. Then she snatched the paper from Linda's hand. "Where does it say that?"

"It doesn't *say* it," Linda explained. "But that's what this paper means. It's a U.S. Origin Health Certificate, and it proves that a horse has had all the shots it needs before it's shipped to another country. I know that because Bronco sent a couple of our horses to England last year."

"Then we'd better get Sheik out of here fast!" Page took hold of the stallion's halter.

Linda reached for the latch on the stall door. But before she could open it, an eerie creaking sound filled the stable.

The girls froze.

A moment later, there was another creak. Only this time they knew what had made the noise.

A rusty door hinge.

"Someone's coming!" Linda whispered. She grabbed Page's wrist and dragged her around the pile of hay. They squatted in a dark corner.

Slowly, the door creaked all the way open. Then muffled footsteps thudded on the dirt floor.

Whoever had entered crossed the stable, then stopped.

Linda held her breath. She could hear Sheik thrashing back and forth in his stall. He pawed the straw and snorted.

There was a sound of scraping metal and a loud clank. The latch! Someone was opening Sheik's door!

"Oh, no!" Page whispered. "They'll see the halter and lead line."

Then the girls heard a click, and a ray of light flickered across the floor. The footsteps moved closer.

"We've got to make a run for it!" Linda touched Page on the shoulder and pointed to the hole at the back of the stable.

Page nodded, then sprang from their hiding place. Linda was right on her heels. They raced across the stable to the hole in the wall where they'd entered. Page ducked and slid through.

Linda glanced over her shoulder. The beam of light

flashed on the pile of hay. Quickly, she stuck her leg through the hole.

Suddenly, a hand clutched her arm and yanked her back into the stable.

"What're you kids doing here?" a gruff voice asked.

The bright beam of a flashlight shone in Linda's face, blinding her. She threw up her hands to shade her eyes. The flashlight clicked off, and, blinking, Linda looked up. Phil was staring down at her.

"Phil?" Linda's mouth fell open in surprise.

Just then Page stuck her head through the opening. "Linda?"

"Yes! I'm here. And so is Phil!" Linda gave Page a hand as she climbed back into the stable.

"Thank goodness," Page said when she caught sight of the trainer.

"What are you doing here?" Phil asked again.

"We were looking for Sheik," Linda explained. "And we followed a truck into the ghost town and found him."

Phil shook his head in amazement. "I guess you girls were right all along. Looks like someone did take him."

"And you should see what the crooks did to my horse!" exclaimed Page. She led Phil over to the stallion's stall.

"We almost didn't recognize him," Linda said.

Sheik greeted everyone with a friendly nicker.

"I'm glad to see he's all right," Phil said, leaning over the stall door to scratch behind the horse's ears. "Though he sure looks different."

Linda looked curiously at Phil. "What are *you* doing here?" she asked.

"Oh, I was looking for Sheik, too," he said quickly.

"Funny how we both found him at the same time," Page said. "I mean, I never dreamed Sheik would be in a ghost town! We only knew he was here because we followed a blue pickup from the . . ."

As Page rattled on, telling Phil how they'd tracked down Sheik, Linda quietly studied the trainer's expression.

He was leaning against the stall, a relaxed smile on his face. But still, Linda knew something wasn't right.

For one thing, he'd said he was at the ghost town looking for Sheik. But how did he even *know* about the place? And why would he think to look for Sheik there?

". . . so I *borrowed* one of your boots and set it by the print, and they didn't match up!" Page took a deep breath, then went on.

The bootprint, Linda repeated to herself. One more thing that didn't add up. Phil had let them think the print was his. Yet Page had proved it wasn't. Why *had* he lied about walking Sheik? Linda wasn't so ready now to accept Page's theory about Phil lying to make them feel better.

". . . and then we noticed that the tires on the truck had the same zigzag pattern!" Page finished with a proud grin.

"That's some story," Phil said, straightening up and looking around the stable.

But why would Phil take the stallion? Linda wondered, suddenly uncertain. She knew he'd never do anything to hurt Sheik.

"I think we'd better get Sheik out of here as soon as possible," Phil said. "Right now, there doesn't seem to be anyone around. Why don't you and Page go out to the jeep—it's parked behind the old jail—and call the ranch on the CB. Bronco can bring the van. I'll wait here with Sheik."

Linda didn't know what to say. It sounded like a good idea, except . . . Oh, she wished Bronco were there! He'd know what to do.

She stepped forward. "Why don't you go radio the ranch," she said to Phil. "And Page and I will stay here."

Phil shook his head. "Too dangerous," he said. "I can't leave you girls alone with Sheik. What if those two men come back?"

"What two men?" Page asked.

"The two men in the truck," Phil said.

"But we didn't say there were two men in the truck," Linda told him.

"I just assumed . . ." His voice trailed off.

Page reached for the latch on the stall door. "Well, I'm not leaving Sheik!"

Phil put his hand out to stop her. "Wait a minute. You're being foolish. He's perfectly safe here with me!"

"Unless you're the one who took him!" Linda blurted out.

Startled by her words, Phil and Page turned and stared at her.

"Linda!" Page exclaimed in disbelief. "What are you saying?"

"I'm saying there are too many things that don't add up. Like why Phil lied about walking Sheik on the road Saturday," Linda said, feeling bolder, but at the same time hoping Phil could come up with a good explanation. "And how he knew about the ghost town. And why he thinks there were two men in the truck."

For a moment, no one said anything. Page and Linda watched Phil, waiting for some answers.

The trainer shifted uncomfortably. He ran a hand through his hair and looked nervously around the stable. "I can explain everything," he said. "But not now. We have to get Sheik out of here." He grabbed for the lead line, but Page jerked it out of reach.

"Not until you answer Linda's questions," she said quietly.

"Look, it was a mistake," Phil said. "A stupid mistake."

"Then it *was* you!" Page said. "But why?"

"I didn't steal him!" Phil protested. "I just got tired of watching you mistreat him. He's too good a horse to let someone like you ruin him."

"Then who did steal him?" Linda asked. "Was it Ralph Greene?"

Phil shook his head sadly. "No. He would have treated Sheik just the same as Page did. Always pushing him to win, win, win. As if nothing else mattered."

"Why didn't you say something to me?" Page asked.

"I *did*. Only you wouldn't listen," Phil said grimly. "So when I got the opportunity to give Sheik to someone who'd love him as much as I did, I jumped at the chance. At the time, I thought it was a good idea. Now I realize how crazy it was . . ."

Page turned to the stallion. Sheik pushed her gently with his nose. "Did I really treat you that badly?" she asked, stroking his neck.

But Linda wasn't quite as touched by Phil's story.

"You still took him," she accused. "Then blamed it on Amber."

"I didn't take him," the trainer replied. "I just set it up."

"Then who did?" Page asked.

Linda's eyes lit up. "I'll bet it was the two men at the show. The men you were talking to."

Phil nodded. "The one guy, Tom Tracey, has a daughter who comes to all the shows. She loves horses, especially Sheik. She used to visit him before the Duvalls bought him."

Linda wasn't sure if she should believe Phil's explanation or not. Something about it didn't make sense. Then she remembered—the health certificate! She'd forgotten about it in all the excitement. If Phil was telling the truth, then why would he need a special permit to send the horse out of the country?

"I don't believe you," she told him suddenly. "Come on, Page. Let's get Sheik back to the ranch. Phil's just stalling so his partners can get here and stop us."

Boldly, she stepped in front of Phil, unlocked the stallion's stall, and swung the door open. She wanted Phil to think she wasn't afraid of him.

But inside her chest, her heart was thumping wildly. While she was talking so bravely, she suddenly realized what big trouble she and Page were in. They were alone, in a deserted town, with a horse thief!

"Easy, boy," she crooned to the stallion. "Let's go." She caught the dangling lead line and clucked to him.

"Hold it!" Phil shut the stall door so they couldn't leave. "You've got to believe me. I want Sheik back at the ranch as much as you do."

Linda handed the lead line to Page. Then she plucked the piece of paper out of her jeans pocket and waved it in the air. "Then how do you explain this?" she said challengingly.

Phil threw up his hands. "Tell me what it is, and I'll explain it."

"It's a health certificate," Linda said. "And it proves you were going to ship Page's horse out of the country!"

For a second, Phil was speechless. Then his face reddened.

"I don't know what you're talking about," he said quietly.

Linda stuck the paper in his hand. He snapped on his flashlight and read it. When he'd finished, all the color had drained from his face.

"I'm so sorry," he said, shaking his head from side to side. "I had no idea. You've got to believe me."

This time Linda did. Phil Granger may have lied about a lot of things, but Linda knew from his expression that the certificate had taken him totally by surprise.

"I believe you," Linda said.

"So do I," Page added.

"What a fool I was," Phil said bitterly. "I really thought that guy wanted Sheik for his daughter. And all along he was planning to sell him!"

"That's right, Granger!" A sharp laugh came from the shadows.

Startled, Linda, Page, and Phil whirled around toward the voice.

A heavyset man stepped from a corner of the dark stable. "You were a first-class fool, and Harrison and I appreciate it."

"Tracey? Is that you?" Phil asked in an angry voice. He clicked on his flashlight and pointed it into the corner.

"It's me." A big man with a beard and squinty eyes stood before them. He held his hand up in front of his face. "Turn that thing off," he growled.

Behind him, the stable doors swung open. The blue truck and horse trailer were parked outside the stable. Another man was opening the back of the trailer. They were there to get Sheik!

Linda glanced at Page and the stallion. Page was staring with frightened eyes at the truck.

"This wasn't part of the deal!" Phil said, holding up the piece of paper. "You lied to me!"

"That's right!" Tracey said. "We figured that was the only way we'd get a valuable horse like him." He nodded toward the stallion. "That little girl's animal is going to make us a bundle of money from a dealer in South America."

"But you can't sell him!" Linda said. "You don't have his registration papers."

"Forged ones are good enough where he's going," Tracey boasted. He chuckled, then narrowed his eyes at Page. "Now, give me the horse, kid, and there won't be any trouble."

Page glanced uncertainly at Phil.

"You'd better do what he says," Phil said quietly. "I don't want anyone getting hurt."

But Linda wasn't about to give up that easily. "No! You can't have him!" she said stubbornly. She pushed past Phil and stood next to Page.

Tracey scowled at her. "You can either hand him over and nothing will happen. Or you can make a fuss and we'll tie you up." He grinned nastily.

"Just try it!" Page said bravely, clasping the lead line even tighter.

Tracey's smile turned sour. "Harrison!" he yelled

over his shoulder. "Get a rope and give me a hand. And be quick about it."

The other man ducked inside the trailer. With a grim set to his jaw, Tracey turned to Page.

"Give me that horse," he demanded, reaching for the lead line.

But Phil was too quick for him.

The trainer slammed the flashlight across Tracey's wrist. Then he knocked into him with his shoulder.

With a cry of pain, the big man stumbled backward.

Phil jumped away from him and turned to the girls.

"Run!" he yelled, giving them both a push toward the door. "Run and get help!"

10 ♦♦♦♦

Linda grabbed Page by the wrist. "Come on!" she shouted.

"I'm not leaving Sheik!" Page cried. She wrenched her arm from Linda's grasp. "Whoa, Sheik! Whoa!" She waved her arms in the stallion's face, scaring him even more.

Linda glanced over her shoulder. The other thief, Harrison, was running toward them.

"Page!" Linda screamed. The blond girl caught the lead line, but it was too late.

"Where do you think you're going with that horse?" Harrison said gruffly. He shoved Page aside. She fell with a thud in the pile of hay.

"Leave her alone!" Linda cried angrily. She launched herself at the man's broad back.

He spun around, throwing her to the floor. Then

he grabbed the dangling lead line and jerked hard on Sheik's halter.

With an angry squeal, the stallion reared. His front hooves pawed the air. The line was wrenched out of Harrison's hand.

He threw his arms up to protect his face from the flailing hooves and lost his balance. He fell over Phil and Tracey, who were still wrestling on the floor.

Linda scrambled to her feet and grabbed Sheik's halter. "Come on, Page!"

Page and Linda raced past the tangle of men. Snorting with excitement, Sheik trotted next to the girls. His neck was arched, and his feet barely skimmed the ground as they ran into the sunlight.

Linda blinked. What should they do? Then it hit her. The horses! They'd ride into the hills where the truck couldn't follow.

"This way!" She waved to Page. They raced behind the barn to the old saloon.

"Take Sheik!" Linda told Page as she ducked under Amber's neck and untied the reins. Then she heard the roar of the truck's motor. The men were coming!

"Quick! Get on Sheik!" she hollered. Dropping Amber's reins, she rushed to the stallion's side.

Page grabbed a handful of mane. Linda took hold

of Page's knee and boosted her onto the stallion's back. Page clutched the lead line with one hand, the mane with the other. She looked scared.

"Just hang on!" Linda shouted encouragingly. Then she vaulted onto Amber's back. Leaning over the mare's neck, she scooped up the reins.

The palomino spun on her hind legs and leaped for the rocky path.

Suddenly, the truck careened around the corner, cutting them off.

Quickly, Linda reined Amber in a circle. They'd have to try another way! She and the mare took off down the alley beside the saloon.

Sheik galloped beside them, Page hugging tight to his mane.

When they reached Main Street, Linda turned the mare toward the dirt road. Maybe they could lose the thieves and get to the gas station. Neck and neck, the two horses raced down the street.

Suddenly, Amber slid to a halt, throwing Linda onto the saddle horn. Linda grabbed a hunk of mane and pushed herself upright. Then she realized why Amber had stopped. The truck had circled behind the buildings and was heading straight for them!

But Page and Sheik hadn't stopped. They were galloping right for the truck. Almost too late, Page caught sight of it. She pulled on the lead line. The stallion wheeled in a circle and charged off in the other direction. But the truck was gaining.

"Over here!" Linda hollered, pointing to a narrow alley. With Sheik on her heels, Amber led the way between the two buildings.

They whirled around the corner and galloped past the old churchyard. The church! Linda thought. They could hide behind it until the truck was farther away. Then they'd make a break for the hills.

She steered Amber around a gravestone to the back of the old building. Sheik skidded to a halt beside them.

Both girls were red-faced and gasping for breath. The horses' necks were lathered with sweat and their sides were heaving.

Linda glanced over at Page, whose cheeks were coated with dust.

Page flashed a brave grin.

Just then the truck zoomed past the church and kept on going. The men hadn't seen them!

"As soon as they're far enough away," Linda said, "we'll cross Main Street and head for the dirt road."

Page gave her the okay sign. They held their breaths and listened. The roar of the motor was growing fainter.

Linda waved Page ahead.

Suddenly, a loud nicker echoed through the town.

It was Smokey Joe calling for his friends. Sheik pricked up his ears, and before Page could stop him, he gave an answering bellow.

Oh, no! Had the men heard it? From a distance came the squeal of brakes, then silence. Linda waited and, at last, let out her breath in relief. But it was too soon to feel safe. The engine started up again. Then its growl grew louder!

"They're coming back!" Linda whispered hoarsely. "We'll never make it across Main Street!"

"We can't stay here!" Page wailed.

Linda racked her brains. Where could they hide? Then she remembered an old shed where she and her friend Kathy used to tie the horses on hot days. If they shut the doors . . . it just might work!

"Follow me!" she called to Page. She urged Amber into a jog. The mare chomped on the bit, eager for another race with Sheik. Linda reined her in firmly but gently.

On the other side of the church, Linda halted the mare and peered around the corner. There was no sign of the truck or the men.

She waved Page over.

Together they cantered across the churchyard to the back of the next building.

"This is the old hotel," Linda whispered. "There's a shed on the other side. Hurry!"

When they reached the shed, Linda looked at the old building in dismay. The tin roof sagged and one wall tilted crazily. She hadn't seen it in over a year, and it had really gotten run-down.

But there was no time to worry about that. She could hear the truck getting closer!

"Come on, Amber!" Leaning forward in the saddle, she let the reins go slack. Cautiously, the palomino stepped through the doorway. Her hoof hit the old plank floor with an echoing thud.

With a snort of terror, Amber reared away from the building.

"Whoa!" Linda pulled her up. This was no time for her horse to act like a filly! "What's wrong with you? Get in there!"

She gripped the reins tightly in both hands and, using her legs, forced the mare forward.

Amber sidled up to the doorway, but refused to go inside.

"Let me ride Sheik in!" Page said. "Then maybe she'll follow."

As Page guided Sheik into the old shed, the thud of his hooves could be heard outside.

Listening to the other horse, Amber danced in place. Suddenly, she plunged into the shed, almost knocking Page off Sheik.

"Whoa!" Linda hollered. She reached down to

reassure the trembling mare. Then she swung her leg around, ready to jump off and shut the doors. But Amber skittered sideways so fast, Linda was thrown back into the saddle.

"Hey!" She grabbed onto the saddle horn.

Suddenly, she heard a sharp crack. The old wooden floor began to groan under the weight of the horses.

Too late, Linda realized what Amber had been telling her. The floor wouldn't hold them!

Amber pinned her ears back and nipped Sheik on the haunch. The stallion turned and lunged out of the shed, Page hanging tightly to his mane.

But the force of his jump cracked the rotten boards in front of the doorway. With a crash, they splintered and fell to the cellar below, cutting off Amber and Linda. They were trapped!

Eyeing the gaping hole, Amber backed deeper into the shed, away from the splintered planks. Linda stared at the opening. It was almost four feet across.

"Whoa, girl." She soothed the mare in a faltering voice.

Maybe if they didn't move, the rest of the floor would hold.

"Linda! Linda!" Page called frantically into the dark building.

"Don't come in!" Linda warned. "Take Sheik and run! Hide him! I'll be all right!"

But it was too late. Linda heard the roar of a truck speeding behind the hotel.

Just then, Amber whirled toward the doorway.

"Whoa!" Linda commanded. But the mare didn't listen. Gathering her powerful legs beneath her, she leaped across the hole and into the sunlight. Linda grabbed the mare's mane tightly and hung on.

"She did it!" Page whooped.

Linda hugged the mare's neck, grinning. But her smile faded when she saw the blue truck round the corner and jerk to a stop.

It was too late to run any more.

Tracey jumped from the driver's seat, his face red with anger.

"Hold it right there!" he growled, jerking the lead line from Page's hand. "Now, get down off that horse. You've had your last ride on him."

"I doubt that," a voice said quietly from the hotel porch.

Linda twisted in her saddle. It was Mac! He was leaning against the wall and smiling as if he didn't have a care in the world.

Harrison opened the truck door and stepped out.

"Oh, yeah?" Tracey said. "And who's going to stop us?"

"I might," Mac said, grinning lazily. Just then, the ranch jeep careened around the corner, blocking the alleyway. "And then again, my friends might," he added as Phil and Bronco jumped from the front seat.

Linda had never been so glad to see anyone in her life.

Tracey and Harrison glanced nervously at each other. Tracey dropped Sheik's lead line, and the two men began backing toward their truck.

But before they could get in, a police car roared up behind them. They were hemmed in.

"Stop those men!" Page cried as Sheriff Garcia got out of the police car. "They're horse thieves!"

"Don't worry, Page." Bronco chuckled. "I think they can handle it."

"These the two men you called us about?" the sheriff asked Bronco.

"That's right, Ed," replied Bronco. "Can you manage them?"

"No problem, Bronco," said Sheriff Garcia. By this time, Tracey and Harrison, realizing they were outnumbered, had given up. The sheriff handcuffed them and shoved them into the police car.

Relieved, Linda watched the police car back up and drive away. It was really over. Sheik was safe.

She steered Amber toward the stallion, caught up his dangling lead line, and handed it to Page.

Page leaned forward and gave Sheik a big kiss.

"Is everyone all right?" Bronco asked.

Linda and Page nodded.

"How's Sheik?" Phil asked, speaking for the first time.

Linda looked at him. He had a black eye and cuts on his mouth and jaw.

"Sheik's great," Page replied. "But what about you?"

"I'm okay," he mumbled from between swollen lips. "They thought I was knocked out." He rubbed the back of his head and grinned. "Fortunately, I'm tougher than I look."

"Phil called from the jeep radio and told us what happened," Bronco explained. Then he looked sternly at Linda and Page. "You two never should have followed that truck alone."

"But—" Page sputtered.

"No buts about it. If it hadn't been for Phil, you'd be tied up in some dark barn, and Sheik would be on his way to Mexico."

Linda looked at Phil, wondering how much he'd told them. He caught her eye, smiled, and nodded.

"Don't worry," he said. "I explained my part in this theft to your grandfather. Later, I'll call Nathan. I'll understand if he wants to press charges."

"I'll talk to Dad, too," Page said to Phil. "I don't

think he'll want to press charges, not after I tell him how you saved our lives."

"Not only that, you didn't let those men take Sheik," Linda added.

"It's a good thing I showed up when I did," Phil said, rubbing his jaw. "Believe it or not, I came here to call off the deal. I'd already decided that what I was doing wasn't the answer."

"Well, it's over now," Bronco said. "And I guess you've been punished enough." He pointed to Phil's bruised face. "So let's just say we all learned something from the experience."

"Well, I've learned never to mistrust Amber again," Linda said. She motioned toward the doorway of the old shed. "I should have listened to her when she didn't want to go in there. We almost fell through the floor!"

Mac, Phil, and Bronco stepped closer to the hole.

Mac shook his head and gave a low whistle. "That must have been a close call," he said.

"And you should have seen Sheik!" Page said, not wanting to be left. "Not only did he knock that man down, he outran a truck!"

"Amazing, isn't it?" Phil said. "Especially since you didn't even have a bridle to control him."

"Or a saddle or whip," Linda added.

"That's right," Page said. She laid her face against

Sheik's neck. "He really is a terrific horse. And to think I almost lost him."

"Well, you have two more weeks at Rancho del Sol," Linda said. "Maybe you can make it up to him."

Page smiled. "I'll try. I know I can be a better rider. Maybe we can even go on some dumb old trail rides," she said to Linda with a laugh. "And if we work real hard, Sheik will be ready for another show before I leave." She gave him a pat. "Even if he never wins a blue ribbon, I think he's the best horse in the world!"

She dismounted and led him over to Phil.

Linda leaned over her saddle horn. "Okay, Amber," she whispered in the mare's ear. "We'll let Page think she has the best horse in the world. But you and I know better, don't we, girl?"

With a toss of her silky mane, Amber nodded in agreement.